Beyond the Past

NIDAL MANSOUR

Beyond the Past

2021 © Nidal Mansour
Publisher: BoD – Hellerup, Denmark
Printing: BoD – Norderstedt, Germany
ISBN: 978-87-4308-325-2

The alarm went off at 5.00 AM. The young professor got out of bed and started his morning routine. It was his first day teaching at the university. He started the day with a few gymnastic exercises after which he took a nice, long shower and then had some breakfast. He had to get everything over and done with before starting work at 8 AM.

Because it was close to his home, he cycled to work. Then he didn't have to worry about the morning traffic or that his car possibly wouldn't start. He showed up at work about 25 minutes early, which meant he had time to prepare. His first lecture was about the universe and he tried to imagine how to start, how to explain things in a way that would capture the young students' attention and not bore them to death. He leaned back in his chair, both hands folded behind his head, contemplating.

The universe was the most unexplored thing in human history. Research was carried out and guesses were made about what Earth would have consisted of millions and billions of years ago. There is so much information to be found in the soil, in the shape of fossils. We find little pieces of bone from creatures we never even imagined walked the earth, we connect the dots and recreate ... KNOCK, KNOCK. Jack was pulled back to the here and now, out of the trance he had been in. Without his say so, the door opened and the Head of University, Mrs Trisseltoft, marched in with her eternally stern looking face. "What should I do with you? Your application was so promising, and you came across as someone whose mind was in the right place!"

Still partly lost in a trance, his brain slowly started working again, like an old car with a cold engine, which had not been used for a long time.

"What time is it?" he slowly mumbled. He knew the answer, because by now, he was wide awake. He jumped up from his chair, squashed the papers into his bag, which he'd thrown on the floor, and stormed out of the stuffed office. He heard Mrs

Trisseltoft shouting from behind, but by then he was already heading down the hallway.

He opened the door to the classroom, where the deafening noise ceased for a moment, but then started again, albeit slightly lower. Jack knew that first impressions were terribly important, and he had already spoilt so many of them. He stood by the blackboard, cleared his throat, but it took several coughs to get the attention of his students. Then he began the important lecture, he had been planning for weeks ...

When his first lecture on palaeontology was over, Jack collapsed in a chair. He had been a palaeontologist for quite a few years now, but having to share his knowledge was new to him. The semester at the university had only just begun, and already his office was filled from floor to ceiling with drawings, diagrams, books and fossils and models related to his work and great hobby: extinct animals from the Jurassic period. For more than a year now, he had been working on a book about these amazing creatures.

He got up from his chair. Fortunately, he did not have to teach any more that day, which meant that he was free to go somewhere else. He knew exactly what he was going to do with the rest of the day. He walked toward the exit of the building and the warm afternoon air enveloped him like a warm blanket.

He felt at home here at the university. There were so many memories from his own student days. However, even back then, the most exciting thing had been his physics professor's lectures. Jack had gotten on really well with him, and they had talked about anything and everything between heaven and earth once Jack had finished whatever chores the professor had asked him to do.

Jack turned around and walked down the narrow hallway that led to the professor's office. There was a warning triangle on his door. Jack knocked four times, slowly but firmly. Nothing happened, and so he opened the door, carefully. The old professor was in his old armchair, his back turned, hunched over a pile of papers with lots of numbers and equations. Finally, the Professor heard him approach, and he turned around in his chair around. His face was aging, marked by fine, deep wrinkles, particularly across his forehead. His hair was longish and grey. Jack knew that he had been a physics professor at the university for more than 40 years. The office was large, only it looked small because of all the stuff gathered in there over the years.

Apart from teaching physics, the Professor also spent his time experimenting and inventing things no one else would even dream of.

"Oh, hi Jack. I thought you might come by. I have a small surprise for you." The Professor smiled widely. "But first, tell me about your teaching, how did it go? Was it challenging? You must never let anything get to you."

Jack looked around the office. He would gladly spend a day studying all the Professor's notes and books. "I'm not sure, I'm really cut out for teaching. And Mrs Trisseltoft does not seem terribly impressed either." Jack sighed and crouched even more in his chair.

The professor's smile widened. "But you know, Mrs Trisseltoft loves brilliant nerds like us, which is also why she's kept me on for so long. You just need to gain her trust. But enough of that! I may have just the thing to cheer you up."

The Professor turned around and walked over to an old cupboard, which had probably been black once upon a time, only now the paint was cracked. He opened it and appeared to be looking for something. Though, from where he was sitting, Jack couldn't see what. Finally, the Professor turned around again. His face was now back in its familiar folds, revealing that something was about to happen. He walked over to Jack and placed an oblong box on the table next to him.

"Open it," the Professor whispered, as he kept a close eye on

Jack's facial expression. Jack picked up the box. It was heavier than he expected, and the size of his fist. He opened the lid and was unable to supress his disbelieving smile. And only when he had picked up the object from the box did he slowly realise what it was. They couldn't be artificial. The four, long yellowish claws, roughly the same length as his hand, shone almost like crystals in the dim light. Jack knew exactly who the claws had once belonged to: Giganotosaurus Tyrannosaurus, one of the greatest carnivores from the Jurassic period, slightly bigger than the famous Tyrannosaurus Rex. Jacks jaw dropped, he couldn't move a muscle.

It was the Professor who broke the silence. "I'm thinking you could use that in your teaching. I guarantee that you won't find specimens more beautiful than the ones you're holding right now." Jack slowly recovered. Stuttered as he asked: "How on earth did you get hold of them? They're in such perfect condition that one would think that you'd recently come across a living specimen."

The Professor immediately withdrew into himself as he slowly responded: "Don't you worry about that. What I can tell you is that it wasn't easy! Anyway, I must be getting on with my research. Goodbye, Jack." He turned his back to Jack and began spreading out some drawings across his desk. Jack knew that asking more questions would be futile, so he got up from the chair, and carefully put the lid back on the box with the valuable claws. Then he said "Thank you," loud and clear as he left and closed the door behind him.

Once Jack was out on the street again, he almost bumped into a young man in a long white coat, who came running along the pavement. He stopped, out of breath, and leaned against the slanting fence. "How is he today? I hope he won't be mad because I'm late."

Jack frowned. He had trouble understanding Rick, who was still desperately trying to drag enough oxygen into his lungs.

"He seemed his usual self, slightly distracted, you know." Rick pushed himself off the fence, which swayed threatening from side to side, and wormed his way past Jack and opened the door. "Nice talking to you, whoever you are, see you later." He closed the door and Jack continued along the pavement, lost in his own thoughts.

It was getting dark as he reached his small apartment. His thoughts hovered around the claws, safely tucked away in their box and in his inner pocket and about the Professor's secretive look. He walked up the narrow stairs and reached the black-painted front door, which opened into his one-bedroom apartment. He fumbled trying to find the light switch.

The second he pressed the switch, something exploded with a deafening noise, or at least that was what Jack thought it sounded like. Way too many people had been crammed into his flat (it felt like a herd and he wondered whether they were even able to even breathe). It wasn't an explosion or a meteorite, just his happy and joyful family. A tall, blond, handsome man welcomed Jack by throwing his arms around him.

"We thought you needed something slightly livelier in your life, not just all those dead dinosaur-friends of yours. Congratulation on your new job. You finally made it!" He threw out his arms, pointing at everyone else in the crowded living room.

His brother had always been the family favourite, with his good looks and his unmistakable understanding of numbers. Now, he was head of the National Bank, and he lived in a great big house with a lovely wife. Yes, James had it all.

His mother approached. "So, Jack, did you have a good day at university? Now that you have a decent job, you'll be able to afford something bigger as well." She gave him a proud smile, something Jack was not used to. His brother, who had overheard his mother speaking, yelled, "All you need now is a nice girlfriend."

A touchy subject for Jack. Everyone who knew him, knew that his love-life had never been easy. His only defence was the tried and trusted: "Yeah, in another world." Which resulted in a gentle laugh from everyone else in the room.

His father was standing at the far end of the room, talking to his mother's sister, Annie. Jack admired his father. His moving business had only recently become successful, and the reason why? So many couples were getting divorced. Only, Jack had never really been a part of his father's dreams. He had not been interested in taking over his father's company. His mother had never judged him, had always said that one should follow one's dreams. And she was the one who had made sure that he was accepted as a palaeontology student, made sure that was able to give it everything he had.

It turned into a late night. Everybody had a lovely time and congratulated Jack on his new job. James left as the last one. "Don't mind what anybody else says, brother. You're just great, even if you do live with a dinosaur." Jack could smell that his brother had probably seen the bottom of a few too many bottles of beer.

In class, the following day, Jack was better prepared. After his guests had departed the night before, he had spent several hours, way past midnight, planning his lecture for the following day. He had discovered that despite his vast collection of palaeontological finds, there were quite a few gaps. However, he would enjoy showing the gawking students the wonderful claws, the Professor had given him the day before.

These rare treasures were the perfect way of getting their attention. He had to pay the Professor a visit to find out if he could provide him with more exciting finds. As soon as the lecture ended, he hurried down the dark hallways until he reached the Professor's office. As always, he knocked first, and as always there was no response. He opened the door, and to his great surprise, the room was empty.

For a brief moment, he wondered where the Professor might be, but his concern was soon replaced by a childish urge to explore the unknown. He walked up to the large desk, littered with piles of papers. Number and drawings that meant nothing to Jack were scribbled on most of the papers. It looked more like hieroglyphs than anything else. He continued browsing through the huge bookcase, next to the desk, and to his surprise he found another piece of paper in the Professor's handwriting, filled with enigmatic numbers and drawings, the likes of which Jack had never seen before. He kept looking ... Then he glanced at his watch.

"Oh, no, I'm going to be late again." He sped out of the room, slamming the door shut behind him. Running down the hallway, he kept thinking about whether the Professor would realise that someone had been in his office, poking their nose around. He briefly thought of the unlocked door ... It was unusual for the Professor to leave his door unlocked.

During the following long lesson, Jack couldn't think about anything but the strange numbers and signs. In his wildest imagination, he couldn't imagine what they meant. He had to ask the Professor, or his curiosity would eat him alive. What did the Professor spend all his time on in that dark office of his? He had often heard other people refer to the Professor as a mad old hatter, but Jack had never agreed. Then again, thinking about the numerous experiments and ideas the Professor was forever working on, it could come across as slightly dangerous. But to call the Professor and inventor mad?

That same night, he dreamt strange dreams. Dreams filled with those damned drawings and numbers, of course. He was studying them when a pair of robot's arms appeared and pulled him into a machine with an open door. The door slammed shut once he was inside and everything turned dark. Suddenly, everything around him turned into the universe. It was as if he floated in infinity. He could see the planets surrounding planet earth and the blazing sun ... With a start, Jack woke from his dream. Was this all happening because he had been snooping around the Professor's office? Was this his punishment? He lay awake for a long time, trying to figure out what the dream meant, but he gave up as the buzzer on the alarm clock went off. He had to put his thoughts to one side and begin a new day. But would he be able to? Perhaps he had better ease his heart and mind and tell the Professor about his snooping around.

When he reached the university, he wasn't able to put the dream aside after all. He simply had to see the Professor, to find out if he was back in his office, if nothing else. Once he finished teaching, he hurried down to the Professor's cave. He held his breath, as he knocked on the door. As usual, there was no response. Jack opened the door and sighed with relief – the Professor was back and Rick who appeared to be the Professor's new protégé, was there as well.

"Ah, there you are, Jack." The Professor turned in his chair and looked at Jack. "I've been waiting for you. There something I would like you to help me with." Jack's mind was racing ahead, while trying to read the Professor's expression. Only Rich and the Professor was in the middle of something, so Jack had to wait until Rich had left. Which fortunately wasn't long.

For a while, neither the Professor nor Jack spoke, they just looked at each other, until the Professor suddenly turned his back to Jack. Jack could no longer contain his guilty conscience.

"I was in here yesterday, snooping around. I would like to apologize for that." The words gushed out with such speed, they fell over one another. The Professor turned to him again, and with a kind expression he asked, "Did you find anything exciting? I heard you, but I was in the toilet."

Jack didn't know what to say, but after a brief pause, the Professor turned around again and started searching through piles of paper. "I know I can trust you, Jack. We've known each other for so long, I want to share my most secret invention with you." He pulled out a piece of paper, which looked like it had been folded many times, and told Jack to come and see him at his home after work. Then he would get all the answers, he was looking for. "Right, well, better get back to my class, and so should you, Jack. See you at lunch."

Jack went back to his own classroom, even though he didn't feel much like it. He would rather know more about what the Professor wanted to talk to him about. When he entered the classroom, he told the students to read pages eleven to twenty-two before lunch, and then write down their thoughts on the subject.

The students weren't happy about the assignment. One of the students was particularly displeased. He spoke funny. He used persons instead of real words. If someone was upset for instance, he would say: "Why are you Trisseltoft?", because Trisseltoft was always upset about something. In this instance, he said that it was "Jack", because he meant that it was boring. However, Jack didn't really care, he was more interested in the Professor's work.

Halfway through the lesson, his brain couldn't cope any longer, so he got up and started writing on the blackboard; the numbers and signs he had seen. One by one, the students raised their heads, giving him and his scribbles funny looks. Jack turned around and told the students to forget what he had said about reading the chapter, instead they should tell him what they thought he had written on the blackboard.

The students were all more than happy to stop reading, and so they began suggesting all sorts of things, including weird things that made absolutely no sense. Jack didn't mind. As long as he could keep his mind occupied until the lunchbreak. When the lesson ended, he went in search of lunch and the Professor. While picking up his lunch, he talked to some of the other teachers, but then the Professor entered and he excused himself and went to join him.

"Hi, Jack, want to keep me company?" the Professor said. "Yes," Jack said with a huge smile. The Professor started talking about his teaching and his students, but Jack was more interested in finding out more about all the other stuff. Only, he didn't want to interrupt the Professor, so he kept waiting for the right moment. When the Professor finally paused briefly, Jack asked him about the mystical numbers and drawings.

The Professor leaned toward him and said that it was not something they could discuss then and there, in front of everyone else. "After all, it's a secret I'm only prepared to share with you." There was nothing Jack could do, other than nod and listen to the Professor talking about his teaching and students, while eating his lunch.

When the lunchbreak was over, he taught some more classes. He asked another group of students if the strange numbers and drawings made any sense to them, but as could be expected, they didn't. Thankfully though, it made the time pass quicker.

Once he finished teaching, Jack was eager to get to the Professor's. He raced his bike down a path leading to the main road. There was a lot of traffic at this hour and the cars queuing up hardly moved at all. Jack was pleased that he'd left the car at home that day. He turned down a sideroad and got to a small street with small houses on both sides. Jack stopped in front of a dark brick house with a black, tiled roof. The Professor's home. The garden in front of the house was growing wild and it kept the light from reaching the house. He had butterflies in his stomach as he rang the doorbell, and the Professor opened the door with an excited smile. He placed one hand on Jack's shoulder and said: "Are you up for seeing something that will change your life for ever?" Inside, the house was exactly as Jack had imagined, with old art on the walls, antique furniture and old wallpaper.

Firstly, they went down into the basement. The Professor told Jack that he had been working on the machine Jack was about to see for almost two decades and now it was finally ready. When they reached the basement, they stepped into a semi-dark office. There were lots of papers, which Jack guessed were part of the experiment. A drawing of a machine caught his attention.

The Professor told Jack that he had always liked him, and when he discovered that Jack was coming to work at the university, he had been overwhelmed with joy, because Jack had always been someone you could trust. "I've been keeping this secret for so long, and not having anyone to share it with has been eating me up. However, then I found out that we'd be working together again," the Professor said and continued to explain that when the government found out that he was working on this invention, they actually chose to help him by building it in a laboratory in Washington DC.

He had been away for a few years, working on a secret project, which unfortunately was closed down once they suspected that someone from the KGB was trying to steal the idea.

"However, once that closed down, I was allowed back at the university to teach a couple of days a week, until retirement," the Professor continued. "They made me promise that I would never talk about it or try to build anything remotely similar without their permission. But it was something I'd been working on for so many years, and that's not something you easily forget. So, this other professor, his name is Doctor Morris, and I decided to secretly continue on our own. Unfortunately, we fell out and so I had to continue all on my own."

Then he led Jack to a bookcase. On the floor next to the bookcase, in the corner where the two walls met, the Professor had built a small door, which was hard to see, even for the Professor, and he had built it. But that was also the point. The Professor opened the small door and typed in something. Suddenly, it sounded as if some of the hinges gave way and loosened their grip on the bookcase. It sounded like the doors of a freight plane opening. After that, shoving the bookcase to one side was easy, and behind the bookcase was another door, which lead to a secret room, which the Professor had also built singlehandedly. The room was insulated with egg trays and there were lots of wires and bright lights.

There was also a machine, which was the biggest thing in there. It was in the farthest, darkest corner and its many luminous buttons sparkled and blinked like there was no tomorrow. The machine was so big a grown man could stand upright inside it. Jack stepped closer to it. He had been waiting for what felt like forever to find out what the Professor wanted to show him. Jack held his breath. He was dying to find out, and he could barely stand still. The Professor closed the door and started punching the luminous buttons. Soon the machine started humming and shaking ever so slightly.

"Right, now it's up and running," the Professor said in a blissful, catlike voice. He faced the machine for quite a while, admiring it, but then he walked over to a bookshelf a few feet away. He picked out four books from the bookshelf and placed them on the floor. Jack caught a glimpse of another hatch inside the wall and he could hear that the Professor was fumbling with a set of keys. A few seconds later, Jack noticed that he put something in his pocket, which was wrapped in red velvet. The he put the books back on the shelf.

He walked back to Jack and pulled out a couple of chairs, so they could sit face to face. Jack opened his mouth, but the Professor raised a finger indicating that he shouldn't speak. Jack was dying to ask so many questions. For a while, they just sat like that, only for Jack, it felt like several hours. Finally, the Professor moved a little. "I've studied and researched many different subjects, anything and everything between heaven and earth, some of it understandable, some of it less so. However, now, I've been able to take it that one step further." He stared into space with the most pensive expression Jack had ever seen in another human being. "Jack, this is my deepest secret, which I have never told anyone. It has taken me approximately twenty years to get to here, to this discovery." Suddenly, a flash of light shot through the Professor's eyes. Jack who had been staring at the Professor was surprised and jumped in his seat. "We have known each other for a long time, and you seem like a trustworthy man in whom I can confide without fear."

Jack's palms were sweating. The thought of the Professor being mad was playing on his mind. "I was about to give it all up, but then I discovered that you were starting at the university, and it gave me hope again. I know that you have a keen interest in the Jurassic period, its greatness and its creatures. This machine will provide you with a better understanding of it all. The Professor looked expectantly at Jack who was lost for words. "Perhaps it sounds quite incredible, but it's a little like being stuck in a computer game."

Suddenly, the Professor stood, and he ordered Jack to follow suit. With stiff legs, Jack followed the Professor to the machine, humming and shining in the far corner. "This is a time machine." The Professor could tell that Jack was a little sceptic. "If you don't believe me, I suggest you take a ride."

Jack didn't know what to do with himself, and he considered whether he was possibly the one person who hadn't thought that the Professor was mad. Perhaps everyone else was right when they said that he was crazy. The Professor was half smiling, waiting for Jack's response. Then he broke the silence by stating that he knew that it was a lot to take in all at once. "It may take you some time to get over the shock. You should go home and think about it until tomorrow."

Jack didn't know what to do. Should he go home, be unable to get it out of his system, perhaps never find out whether or not what the Professor said was true? Or should he take a chance? And as he suddenly had a flashback to the claws the Professor had given him, he knew that he wanted to try it. If not, it would eat him up, and he wouldn't be able to fall asleep. So, he looked the Professor deeply in the eyes and said: "I'm ready when you are."

The Professor clapped his hands, stepped up to the machine and said: "The most important thing to remember is that you're not invincible, and you should stay away from danger and not get mixed up in anything. Watch and observe!" he grabbed a round metal disk with buttons and a small screen, padding it like it was a dear, young child.

"And this disk? It's your ticket back here. Guard it with your life! The only thing you have to do is set the time and date to the same time and date that you left here, and then press the red button. Otherwise, you won't come back, you know. However, should the KGB or the press find out, everybody would want to go back in time and possibly alter something they regret, or they'll want to change the course of history. And this can never be allowed! You have to promise me not to say a word."

Jack had been in a dreamlike state, and he couldn't quite fathom what was happening. He slowly looked around. There was not much room inside the machine. He could just about stand upright, and there was no room to manoeuvre. A shiny, hot lamp shone directly on his dark brown hair and made him break into a sweat, small beads or water popping out all over his forehead. The sides, ceiling and floor were covered in thick, soft, red cloth.

Jack's thoughts now hovered around what the Professor had told him. It made absolutely no sense whatsoever. It was as far out as anything could be. He remembered every horror and war film he had ever watched. He thought about scenes where victims were locked inside a coffin or a fridge, dying a slow death. Was this his punishment for snooping around the Professor's office? It was not as if he had stumbled across some great secret. The noise grew louder and louder, until it was so loud, Jack couldn't finish a thought.

With a huge bang, Jack fell on the soft ground. Suddenly, the machine stopped, after what felt like several hours. Now, everything was quiet. The light in the ceiling was switched off and everything turned dark. He slowly opened his eyes and got back on his feet, taking in his surroundings. This wasn't right, it was nothing like the world he came from. The machine which he had entered in the Professor's home was nowhere to be seen. It was boiling hot beneath the oversized sun, which looked like it had moved closer. The air was thick and damp and there was a smell of rotting wood. However, what fascinated him more than anything was the wonderful vegetation.

There were exotic plants everywhere, plants he had never seen or heard of before. A few resembled plants in his own garden, which were also very rare. For several minutes, he just stood there, looking at the green, rainforest-like landscape. Suddenly, it dawned on him. The Professor had mentioned something about the Jurassic period. It couldn't be, surely. The Professor wouldn't have the means to create an entire scenery like this just to fool or annoy him? Jack decided that he might as well try and find a way out of the forest. Everything around him was different, even the damp air felt strange. Birds and insects made their presence felt as he walked through the forest.

Jack had walked for more than an hour without any hint of a door or any other type of exit and as he continued his search, he heard a rattling noise a few metres from his feet. He looked in the direction of the sound and noticed a nest. Or at least that was what it looked like. In the nest were oblong eggs the size of ostrich eggs. They were light blue with black spots. Jack wanted to get back home to find out more about how it was possible to make fake eggs that looked so real.

Suddenly, he heard trickling water, and straight away, he set off in search of the source. At a distance, he saw a small creek with pure water, but then he froze. He had noticed something moving by the creek. He was too far away to see what kind of creature it was.

Then the ground beneath his feet starting shaking and Jack caught a glimpse of a huge creature running out from the bushes at high speed. The large creature scooped up the smaller creature by the creek, which had not been fast enough. It swallowed the prey in one mouthful and then drank from the creek.

Jack was petrified. From where he was standing, he had a clear view of the huge carnivore, but he couldn't for the life of him remember its names. However, he was certain of one thing; it was a dinosaur.

It finally dawned on Jack, where he had ended up. This was not a game or a dream, it was real. Suddenly, the huge dinosaur turned and focused its tiny, yellow eyes on him. Jack took a steep back and this was enough to reawaken the carnivore's hunting instinct.

Adrenaline kicked in and Jack started running. He didn't know exactly what or whom he was running from, but he ran as fast as he could, backtracking from where he had come. He could hear the huge creature closing in on him from behind. He looked around but recognized nothing. He had to find somewhere to hide fast, a cave or something similar, where no one would be able to find him or reach him and then he would be able to press the small, round disk. Fortunately, the vegetation worked to his advantage as he slid in and out between the tall trees and dense scrubs. He took a sharp right turn and crawled under a tree trunk that had fallen to the ground. The creature continued straight ahead, unaware that he was no longer in front of it. Even when it was quite far away, he could still feel the weight of it as he ground reverberated with each of its step.

Jack stayed underneath the tree trunk for a while. The fear of being someone else's prey still held his body in a tight grip.

Then he took out the disk, set the date and time and pressed the little red button.

With a jolt he was on the floor back in the dark office. He slowly opened his eyes. His back was sore from lying there. He lifted his head and looked around. He noticed the Professor who was in his chair looking at him. It took a while before Jack was able to stand up. The Professor stood and stretched out his arm to help Jack get up. He smiled mystically.

"Pleased to see that you're coming around. The first journey is always the physically most challenging, but you'll get used to it, don't worry." With the Professor's help, Jack managed to sit down on a chair. He couldn't remember much and therefore had no idea what the Professor was talking about. Suddenly though, the memories started flooding his brain. Now, he remembered everything.

"What was that place? You owe me an explanation."

"Yes, well, Jack, I've continued my research, inspired by other people's guesswork and ideas, and I have brought it to a completely new level! I've been working on this my whole life. And even if I do say so myself, I believe that I have arrived at a great result! What you experienced Jack, was time-travel, in your case, back to the Jurassic period. A choice I hope did not disappoint you."

The Professor smiled expectantly.

"Was that how you got a hold of those claws? By travelling back in time?"

Jack wasn't entirely convinced that he was getting the right explanation, but he knew now that it was no accident that he had been given the beautiful claws.

"Jack, you have to understand that you cannot breathe a word of this to anyone. We're done for today."

The Professor swirled his chair around. Jack had so many questions but he knew that he might as well give up for now. The Professor had spoken!

As he walked home that evening, he did not know what to do with himself. He barely slept a wink all night. Everything he had been through passed through his mind. When he awoke the next morning, he wasn't sure whether it had all just been a dream or whether it was real.

Eventually, he managed to get out of bed. He took his time getting ready and he was running terribly late. In fact, he was late for his first lecture. The next few hours dragged along and he found it hard to concentrate. He gave his students assignments they could solve on their own, saving him the chore of teaching. Today, his mind was filled with the memories of the previous day.

When he finally finished teaching, he packed his stuff and went to see the Professor. He needed some answers. And as the Professor was not at the university, he had to seek him out at his home. Jack knocked several times before the Professor came to the door.

"Not too afraid to come back, I see. Considering what you went through. Makes a lot of people think they've gone mad. Then again, you don't look like you've slept much."

Jack who only minutes ago had been bursting with questions was at a loss for words. He didn't know what to say. For a long time, he just sat there while the questions simmered on the inside. Eventually, the Professor spoke.

"If you're interested, you can go again."

That was an offer Jack had not expected to get. He hadn't even considered the possibility of going back, of experiencing that amazing rush again. Yet, at the same time, he was well aware that going back and forth in time could not be entirely risk-free. And so, all his questions resurfaced and they tumbled out, disorderly and rapidly, and in the end, even Jack couldn't quite follow his own train of thought.

"I understand that you have so many questions, but it would

take me a lifetime to explain. The most important thing for you to know is that changing things in the past can be very dangerous. Leaving things as they are can be challenging, which is also why it's important that no one else discovers what this wonderful machine can do."

The Professor stopped talking and glanced at the huge machine tucked away in the corner.

"I trust that you of all people understand. Imagine if you could go back in time and change events. Everything evil that has already happened. Which is also why it's imperative that you do not change a thing when you go back in time. And now it's time for you to leave. I have lots to do. Think about what I told you and decided whether or not it's something you would like to try again."

The Professor opened the door and reluctantly, Jack left. He still had lots of unanswered questions burning a hole in his brain, only he knew that there was no point in pestering the Professor further. He turned homeward and decided to write his experiences down. He already sensed the increasing vagueness of his memories. It was probably because of his travelling back and forth in time.

Once he returned to in his small, untidy apartment, which he had had no time to neither tidy or clean since the Professor set his mind spinning because of the time machine, he sat down and commenced writing notes. Even though Jack had a job, it didn't pay well, not least because he was young and inexperienced. He had always dreamt of expanding his field of knowledge to a higher level, which would secure him a decent wage as well. He was fed up with always having to make do, but at the same time he felt like he was stuck in a hole. Again, he started thinking about what had happened to him in recent times. All the things that felt like a dream, could they be his ticket to a better life, filled with fame and fortune? He wondered if the Professor would send him back in time again.

When he went to bed that night, a myriad of thoughts fluttered around his head. He knew that he would have to come up with a plan to benefit as much as possible from the situation. It was like being in a live dream. He wasn't sure if he dared go to sleep. What if he would then wake up only to discover that it had all been nothing more than a wonderful dream.

The day dragged on and Jack couldn't concentrate because of the noisy young students. However, when the last lesson was over Jack livened up again. He tried to keep a modest tempo as he walked toward the university exit, but once he was out of sight, he cycled as fast as he could down the busy streets leading to the Professor's house. He knocked on the solid wooden door and entered the house. The Professor must have been expecting him. He was in his armchair facing the door, hands folded across his stomach.

"I thought I might be seeing you today. Are you ready for another trip to the past?"

Jack nodded.

"I'm not quite sure how to prepare for such a journey, but it's an offer I cannot refuse."

The Professor rose from his chair and went down to the room with the machine. He set the timer at "Jurassic 200,000" and pressed the red accept button. Jack got in and closed the heavy door tightly. However, it was soon reopened by the Professor.

"Now, remember Jack, don't change anything. You can watch, but you must keep your distance."

He closed the door again. There was a loud noise, which he also remembered from last time. He was convinced that everything was going according to plan. The machine stopped shaking and suddenly, everything went quiet. Like last time, the damp heat almost knocked him over. He looked around. Fortunately, he was in a forest again, but to make sure that the disk would not be exposed to curious dinosaurs' jaws, he glued it to his body and placed both hands tightly around it.

There were no signs of life, apart from the varied vegetation. This time, he paid much more attention to everything around him. He hardly knew where to look. He did not want to miss out on anything. He gathered egg shells from hatched eggs, stones and everything else he could get his hands on, and which he believed would cause no harm in the future.

Jack looked at his wrist watch. Going by the belief that it still worked in the past, it revealed that he had been in the magical world for more than four hours. He had done nothing but wander through the enormous forest. Fortunately, he had only encountered less dangerous dinosaurs, who had been busy examining giant insects on the forest floor. Finally, he took out the disk he had glued to his body and typed in the date and time before pushing the red button.

When he arrived back in his own time, he had no problems exiting the machine by himself. He was not thrown to the floor like last time. But just like the last time, the Professor was in his armchair watching him. Jack sat down on an available chair.

"So, Jack, was everything as wonderful as you remembered it?" He folded his hands behind his head.

"It was much better than I remembered ..."

Jack talked for more than ten minutes about his amazing experiences and the Professor just sat there quietly listening. When Jack finally reached the end of his tale, the Professor got up from his chair and picked out a book from the vast bookcase. He returned to his armchair and handed Jack the book.

"I think you should have this book. Have a read, and you may well find inspiration for your next journey. What do you say, same time tomorrow?"

It was a question Jack had longed to hear. The thought of not being able to go back to that amazing world again was terrible. Jack thanked the Professor for the book and headed home. It was dark now, and there wasn't much traffic.

He switched on the light in his apartment and sat down on the sofa. He took out the things he had brought back from the past and examined them. After a while, he opened the book and started to flick through the pages. It was an old book, Jack realised. The pages were yellowish and the language was old-fashioned and not easily comprehensible. He kept flicking through the pages, enjoying the beautiful and colourful images.

When Jack woke up, his entire body was aching. He had fallen asleep on the sofa, which was way too small to fit all of him on there. He looked out of the window. The sun was already up high in the sky. Jack knew exactly what he wanted to do on this the first day of the weekend. He knew he shouldn't really disturb the Professor, he would most likely also enjoy some time off. And they had already arranged to meet later on in the afternoon.

He had breakfast and dressed himself in green from top to bottom. Then he jumped in his old Ford and stopped in a parking area twenty minutes later. Then he opened his oblong case and took out his rifle. Holding it in his hand, he felt like he could accomplish anything in the whole wide world and all his thoughts and worries were put to one side.

The first series of clay pidgins was launched and Jack fired three shots, spot-on each time. Once he had completed all ten series, he packed his bags and drove to the Professor's house. He stepped out of the car and remembered to bring his rifle. The overgrown house looked dark, but they were supposed to meet up shortly.

Jack walked up to the front door and knocked. There was no answer, so he carefully tried the handle and the door opened. The Professor was nowhere to be seen.

"Professor?"

Jack closed the door after him and looked around.

"I'll be up in a minute," came the Professor's voice from the basement.

Jack had a wander around, looking at all the wonderful books lined up in the huge bookcase, then at the equations written in chalk on the green board. He walked over to the desk, which was filled with papers and files. He sat in the chair, across from the Professor's armchair.

Jack could tell that the Professor was worried as he emerged from the basement, and so he asked him what was bothering him. The Professor explained that a few years ago – after the project was cancelled and before he managed to get the time machine up and running – he had worked with another professor, as previously mentioned. Once the project was cancelled, they had decided to continue their work in secret, but halfway through, they had had a huge argument. Before the Professor resigned the other professor had sworn to have his revenge and had made some serious threats, including getting the CIA to take a closer look at what he was up to. Since then, the Professor had not heard from his former colleague.

"But I've seen him a few times, on the street, here in town, which puzzles me, because he doesn't live her. There's no knowing whether it was by accident or if he's spying on me, waiting for the right moment to blow the whistle on me. It's been quite a while since the last time I spotted him, but if he's still alive, and if he ever found out, it would be a disaster. It's one thing if the machine ends up in the hands of the wrong people and is used for bad rather than good things. It is quite another if Russia or China get their hands on it. Then the US would soon cease to exist."

The Professor sunk into his chair and started rubbing his eyes.

"It's incredible that you can invent something as magical as this and still be sad and depressed. I should have spent my time trying to come up with a cure for cancer. Then everybody would have been happy. Including me. However, unfortunately, I'm a physicist and not a doctor, and I'll just have to live with that."

The Professor leaned forward and continued:

"I know you'd like to try it again, but there are too many thoughts in my head. There have been ever since I got the time machine up and running. And they won't go away. On the contrary, it only gets worse the more I think about it, piling bad thoughts on bad thoughts. What I would like you to do, Jack, is help me find Dr Morris. He moved away shortly after our fight, and since then I've been trying to find out what he's up to, but so far, I haven't succeeded. Perhaps you'll do better than me."

The Professor rose from his chair and went to look at his books.

"And now I want to read a good book so I can unwind. You must promise me that you'll find Dr Benjamin Morris. His last known address was 69, Maple Road. Until then, we must keep quiet about travelling back and forth in time."

Jack got up and gave the Professor a hug as he promised that he would do everything he possibly could to find Dr Morris. Then he left. The first thing he did once he arrived home was switching on his computer to search for Professor Morris.

Several hours later, he still had no information. Jack couldn't understand how each search came up empty. Dr Morris had literally become invisible. Jack looked around his apartment, noticed how messy it was and said:

"Well, since I'm not going back to the Jurassic period, I might as well do a bit of tidying."

Jack had not had much time to work out or clean his apartment lately because he'd been so absorbed by the Professor's time machine.

The next day, Jack woke and began his usual morning routine. Then it was time for his family visit, which was a Sunday routine. Jack loved his family and loved spending time with them, even if they were a little crazy.

After a long, lovely shower, Jack put on some nice clothes and drove the hour it took to get to his parents', not counting any breakdowns along the way. When he arrived, he received a warm welcome, as always.

"Dinner's nearly ready, we're just waiting on your brother."

His brother was always the last one to arrive, because he spent so much time getting his children ready. After dinner, they all sat and talked about any news in their lives, but Jack didn't tell them much. He talked about how hard it was to maintain his students' attention and never mentioned that he had had the most exciting week of his life and that he'd had the most mind-blowing experience one could ever dream of. Only, he couldn't talk about it, so he spent most of the time listening to everyone else. Jack rose from his chair to get something to drink from the kitchen, where his mother was busy filling up the dishwasher.

"Something is bothering you," his mother said. Jack shook his head with a fake smile.

"A mother always knows when her child is worried by something," she continued, but Jack insisted that it was merely his new job which was taking its toll. His mother looked at him and said that if he didn't want to talk to her, he should try talking to his father or his brother. When suddenly it dawned on him that as James worked in a bank, perhaps he could get him information on Dr Morris. He kissed his mother and thanked her, and then went looking for his brother.

Jack took James aside and asked him whether he would be able to dig up some information on a person. James smiled and said: "Is it a girl?"

"No, Jack said. "It's a professor I would like to get in touch with, because he might be able to help out with some research issues."

"It won't be easy," James said. "Because it's illegal and furthermore, you'll need his civil registration number." Despite the illegality involved, James was willing to do anything for his family. Jack gave him a huge hug and thanked him and then both of them went to join the rest of the family.

However, even though Jack loved spending time with his family, he could barely keep still. He was eager to see the Professor to find out if he had the vital information needed. As the night wore on, the children were getting tired and everybody headed home. Jack thanked his parents for a lovely day with wonderful food and kissed them goodbye.

As he was leaving, his father told him to just take it easy and hang on in there. "Teaching is only tough for about a hundred years." Everyone laughed and said: "Who lives to be a hundred?" as they got in their cars.

Jack hurried over to see the Professor to ask if he had the required information about Dr Morris. "I hope he's not sleeping when I get there," Jack thought to himself. The house looked dark on arrival, but Jack decided to knock on the door anyway. A few seconds later the Professor opened the door.

"I was afraid you'd gone to bed already," Jack said.

"Oh, no, no," the Professor said. "I was just down in the basement." After which they both went down there. Jack was shocked at what he saw. The time machine had been more or less completely dismantled.

"Don't worry," the Professor said. "I can put it back together again with my eyes closed. I just want to make sure no one else can use it, till we know more about what happened to Dr Morris."

"Well, I may have some good news," Jack said. "Would you by any chance happen to have Dr Morris' civil registration number? It would help a lot."

The Professor dropped what he had in his hand and sat down on one of the chairs. It was quiet for a moment. Then he said: "Actually, I might have some information."

After a couple of hours searching for additional information on the doctor, he Professor said that it was getting late and that Jack ought to go home and get some sleep.

"We can talk tomorrow, at the university, and hopefully, I'll be able to give you more information on Dr Morris."

Jack picked up his things and drove home. Fortunately, he was so tired he fell asleep as soon as his head hit the pillow.

The next morning, Jack got up and did his morning routine as he always did. Then he cycled to work. When he arrived at the university, the Professor was not in his office. But then again, Jack was early and so he went to the staff room where he bumped into the last person he would want to: Mrs Trisseltoft. Fortunately, though, she seemed happy.

"So, Jack, how was your first week?"

"It's been great, thanks," he said. "And I look forward to spending a lot of time with the young people, sharing my knowledge with them."

"I'm very pleased to hear that, Jack," Mrs Trisseltoft said. "Carry on the good work."

Jack let out a sigh of relief and continued toward the staff room. Still no sign of the Professor, so Jack started preparing the day's first lesson and chatted with some of the other teachers. Then it was time to teach and they all went their separate ways.

As soon as Jack entered the class room, he started talking about his favourite subject: dinosaurs. The students were completely absorbed and soon they began asking interesting questions. Halfway through the lesson, the Professor showed up. Jack made excuses and joined him in the hallway.

"Here," the Professor said. "This is all the information on him I could find. Use it sensibly."

Jack returned to the class room and continued teaching. But when it was his lunchbreak, he called his brother immediately and gave him all the information he had. James promised to find out as much as he could and get back to Jack as soon as possible.

After lunch, Jack continued teaching, and once the lessons were over, he went to see the Professor to tell him that he was waiting on his brother's phone call. It was nearly 4 PM and still Jack hadn't heard anything from James. But then he called, and James had good news to share.

"We got lucky. Dr Morris is one of our clients," James said and then shared all the information he had with Jack. Then he went to see the Professor to let him know about the progress. They talked about how to move forward without Dr Morris finding out and getting suspicious.

That evening, they drove the Professor's car past Dr Morris' house to check if the information they had received was also correct. Having found a secluded place to park the car, the Professor grabbed his binoculars and looked at the windows of the house. Within minutes he saw Dr Morris as he passed one of the windows.

"That's him!" the Professor shouted, giving Jack a shock. The Professor put the binoculars down, started the car and drove home. On the way, they talked about whether or not they should try to find out if Dr Morris was still on the prowl, if he was looking for revenge. The Professor promised he would find out more the next day.

Once they arrived back at the Professor's, Jack got on his bike and cycled home. Once there, he watched some television; he wanted to distract himself and think about other stuff until he felt tired and fell asleep.

The next day was similar to every other day, until lunchtime, where he and the Professor exchanged a few words, agreeing that Jack should come and see him at his house after work, and then they could plan their next step.

So, after the day's work was done, he went to see the Professor and make plans. They both had ideas, but decided that it would probably be better if they tailed Dr Morris for a few days to find out more about what he was up to, and only then could they plan further ahead.

Back home again, Jack was relaxing when a man came to see him. "Why are you following me?" the man asked. Jack couldn't tell who he was, until he came a little closer, and he realised that it was Dr Morris.

Jack was speechless. He felt like he'd been struck by lightning, his entire body was paralyzed. He didn't know how to respond.

"Yes, well, when you notice a car that you've never seen parked near your house before, you check it out," Dr Morris said. Jack played ignorant and said that he had no idea who the man was. Then he took a big risk by inviting the man inside for a cup of coffee if he felt like telling Jack what this was all about. Dr Morris accepted the invitation and followed him upstairs. Jack kept fairly quiet, pretending to know nothing, and that way he got Dr Morris to tell him everything.

He told Jack that he and the Professor were old friends and one day they decided they would try to build a time machine. However, halfway through the project, his wife was in an accident and died.

"I told the Professor that when we had finished building it, I wanted to try and go back so I could save my wife. But that freaked the Professor out and he started talking about how we shouldn't change the past. But quite honestly, nobody knows what will happen, it's only guesswork. Nobody has ever succeeded in building a time machine, travelled back in time and changed anything, which completely changed the world. We would be the first and only ones who would do this, so why not try? Which is why I've been keeping an eye on the Professor to see if he would continue the project or not. And the reason he never found out that I was watching him is because I am and always will be smarter than him. Which is why you never saw me, but I saw you."

Jack couldn't really say much, except that he knew the Professor from his university days and he had visited him a few times to help him with various assignments. Dr Morris looked at him suspiciously, drank the rest of his coffee in one mouthful, got up from where he was sitting. He thanked Jack for the coffee and apologized for wasting his time. Then he left.

Jack who had hoped for a quiet evening in, now realised that it had just turned to hell. He didn't know what to do. Should he tell the Professor or should he lie? Or should they let Dr Morris participate in the project, because somewhere along the line, he was right. Who knew whether time travel would affect the future in any way? Nobody had tried it yet. It was all guesswork. He would have to sleep on it and then decide on what to tell the Professor in the morning.

The next morning, Jack rose and while finishing his morning routine, he couldn't help but think about what would happen if he said the wrong things to the Professor. Maybe it would freak him out and he would end up destroying the machine, and then he would never be able to go back and study the Jurassic period again, which he had looked so much forward to.

There were so many things to be explored and experienced. It felt like one lifetime would not be enough. When Jack arrived at work, he tried to avoid the Professor as much as he could, until he decided what to do. When the lunchbreak was over, he stayed in his class room and finished some work he had not yet had time to complete. However, after only a few minutes, the Professor entered the room. He was very distraught.

"Where have you been all day?" he said in a worried tone of voice. Jack told him that he had lots of things that he needed to catch up on. "Oh, well, never mind," the Professor said. "I've found a way for us to get close to Dr Morris without him finding out."

Jack didn't know what to say, other than restating the fact that he was so far behind on his work because of all the time they had spent together.

"I really don't want to upset Trisseltoft and risk being sacked," Jack said with a false smile.

"Okay, then. We can just meet back at my place, once we're done here." The Professor said.

Jack nodded and smiled. He was relieved that it gave him another couple of hours to consider what to tell the Professor. However, when he had finished teaching for the day, he still didn't know what to say to the Professor, and so he decided that he would just listen to whatever the Professor had to say.

When Jack arrived at the Professor's house, he looked around to see whether anybody was watching him as he slowly made his way to the front door. He knocked. The Professor opened the door and placed his hand on Jack's shoulder.

"Come on in, my boy."

Jack glanced back over his shoulder to make sure that nobody was watching, before entering. Immediately, the Professor explained to Jack that he should bump into Dr Morris by accident, carrying a book that he knew Dr Morris liked and then hope that he would then approach Jack.

When he finished, Jack asked him about Dr Morris, about what kind of man he was and why they had fallen out and gone their separate ways. The Professor told Jack the same story as Dr Morris had, only from his perspective. And so, Jack felt obliged to ask him the same question Dr Morris had asked him, about how he could be so positive that changing the past would affect the future.

He posed the question to see how the Professor would react, only the Professor said it was a matter of logic: if you change the past, it will affect the future.

"But surely, people living in our current times won't change simply because you change something in the past," Jack said. "And what about the fossils you brought back?"

"They are dead things, nobody held a funeral, there's no family still alive," the Professor responded.

Jack had to agree with what the Professor was saying, because it sounded convincing, and furthermore, he was the one with the time machine. Before Jack left, he told the Professor that if they were going to tail Dr Morris, they should make sure that he wasn't tailing them. Just to be on the safe side.

Jack was exhausted when he arrived back home. He couldn't

stop thinking about what he had gotten himself mixed up in. The following day, he felt more and more convinced by the Professor's point of view. It was also a must if he wanted to experience the high from time travelling again.

However, none of it would be allowed to affect his work, so he decided to keep work and private life separate. At the university, he only talked to the Professor about matters relating to their work, and he left everything else for after hours. When he finished teaching, he finished whatever else he had to do, and only then did he see the Professor in his basement.

Jack had decided that he would try to get in touch with Dr Morris, only before he left, he made the Professor promise that he would not follow him and risk exposure.

Jack went by bus and train, and within a couple of hours, he was in front of Dr Morris' house. Once inside, Jack tried to convince Dr Morris that there was nothing happening in the Professor's life. Only work. And perhaps, he had been the one to continue working on the time machine?

Dr Morris did not look convinced and told Jack that he was more than welcome to have a look around, to see if he could find any signs indicating that he had a time machine.

Before leaving, Jack told Dr Morris that he should stay away from him and the Professor, and if failing to do so, Jack would tell the police if he ever saw him anywhere near them.

Then Jack hurried back to the Professor. He was convinced that Dr Morris was watching him and he sincerely hoped that the Professor wouldn't freak out and destroy the machine.

When Jack arrived at the Professor's house, it was already getting dark. He was not going to waste any more time, he would tell the Professor straight up that he was being watched. The Professor opened the door and immediately, Jack could see that he was up to something. He sincerely hoped that it did not include destroying the machine. Once inside though, he was relieved to see that the Professor was in fact putting it back together again.

Jack told the Professor that Dr Morris knew who they were. "We're being watched."

"It doesn't surprise me," the Professor said. "And it won't stop me from fulfilling my mission. You go home and get some rest, Jack. Then come back tomorrow and prepare yourself for another journey. We should get as much as we possibly can out of the machine, before someone finds out what we're up to and we lose the machine."

Jack went back home and started thinking about what to bring on his next journey, and what to bring back, because he had decided on a strategy, once he returned to the Jurassic period; he wanted to make sure he made the most of it, not least because every trip could very well be his last.

The following day, Jack was more than well prepared, and he could hardly wait until it was time to go to the Professor's. Jack did everything he could to make the day fly by faster. At 4 o'clock, Jack was the first one out of the door.

When he arrived at the Professor's house, the Professor could tell that he'd not had much sleep, he looked a little tired, but he was still raring to go. The Professor started punching various buttons, and Jack stepped into the time machine, noticing the by now well-known pull in his stomach. He waited as the sounds grew louder. And suddenly, he realised that it was taking a bit longer than the last time. He started to think back ... No, he was convinced that the increasing noise was lasting longer this time. He started to feel claustrophobic, locked inside such a small space. The noise was getting louder and louder, and in the end, he had to pop his fingers in his ears, although it wasn't easy. The noise kept rising nonetheless, and as if that wasn't enough, the machine also started shaking violently. Jack felt his stomach turn. With a huge bang, the lights went out and Jack fell out of the machine and landed on his stomach, on soft grass.

He regained consciousness without any idea of how long he had been knocked out. He lay on the grass, eyes closed and inhaled the smell of succulent, newly mowed grass. As he lay there enjoying the lovely smell, one tiny braincell tried to tell him that it was all wrong. With a jolt, he lifted his head and opened his eyes wide. The first thing that caught his attention was a small house only a few metres away.

What went wrong? raced through his head. He got up on his feet and looked around. There were a dozen houses scattered around, all of them with beautifully kept gardens out in front. Streets and pavements wound prettily in and out between the houses. Behind the small village, he could see a green blanket of trees. The sun was shining, the sky was blue. Jack sighed with relief. He had ended up in his own world.

He straightened his shirt, which had become crumpled while he slept, and walked over to the nearest pavement. He had to find the Professor's house quickly to see if he had left any traces. Maybe he would have time to cover them up, before the Professor noticed that he'd pressed buttons he shouldn't have, possibly even wrecked the machine.

He looked at the street signs. It took a while before he realised ... that he couldn't read them. It was a foreign language, without letters he could recognize. His immediate thought was that he was in some Middle Eastern country. But he had actually studied several languages and this was nothing like any of them. Then it dawned on him: they look like runic letters. Only, that made no sense at all, because the Vikings had not had lovely brick houses with well-trimmed gardens. Then the first human being showed up. He let out a sigh of relief. The young woman walking towards him looked like a normal person, no axe and no unkempt hair. He smiled at her in a friendly manner, as she passed him on his left side, only she stared straight ahead without even noticing him.

Then Jack decided that he had probably hit his head so hard during the rough ride and that was why he couldn't read the signs properly. He continued along the neat pavement. A young boy was heading in his direction. Jack examined him quite closely to see if there was something odd about this boy. He didn't even notice Jack, he too continued straight ahead. Jack continued walking, now in search of the university.

Everything around him seemed so familiar, yet unrecognizable. Jack kept wandering down twisting streets lined by well-kempt gardens and villas. He reached one of the larger and busier roads, where there were lots more people and shops, but again, everything looked different. Then some sort of car showed up, a make he had never seen before. It was heading toward a big road and suddenly, two robotic arms emerged on either side of the car. Apparently, they fit into two holes on the side of the car, obviously designed to pick it up and place it on some kind of reversed conveyer belt. Looking further down, he saw lots more cars on the reverse conveyer belt. This can't be right, Jack thought to himself. The Professor must have sent me to the future. Jack started walking back towards the place he came from, because he wanted to return to his own time.

Then again, he couldn't help but wonder what the future would be like. Jack stopped and considered the fact that he would probably never get a chance like this again to peek into the future, so he walked over to a woman who was waiting at a bus stop and said: "Excuse me, could you point me in the direction of Harvard University?"

At first, the woman didn't even respond, she just kept looking for her bus. Slowly, she turned her head around to face Jack, giving him a suspicious look. Jack's first thought was how long it had been since he had been out in the streets interacting with current culture. She opened her mouth, but it was as if she wasn't sure what to say.

Then a torrent of foreign language fell out of her mouth, it sounded blissful with a delicate touch of music. However, judging by her tone of voice, she was obviously very annoyed with his presence. Before Jack had time to react, an unexpected noise rose above the village. A sound Jack could not relate to anything he had previously heard of heard of. It was short notes of high-pitched sound, and it would appear to be some sort of alarm. Startled, Jack looked to the sky, as it sounded like the noise came from the clouds drifting around up there. The noise reminded him of a mixture of crazy bird cries and loud thunder.

None of the people around him reacted, a few glanced up at the sky and rapidly moved on. Again, Jack looked at the sky and he had to rub his eyes, because on the horizon, it would appear that a gigantic screen was silently being pulled across the town, eventually covering it completely. The big roof was transparent, which meant it only blocked a few of the sun's rays, and more than anything, it felt like a giant cloud. Jack ran across to a young woman as she was passing, he grabbed her by her arm.

"What's going on?" he shouted despairingly as he imploringly looked at the young woman with long, brown hair. She gave him a frightened look and wrenched her arm out of his grip while shouting. She spoke a language, Jack was quite sure he had never heard before. Which country was this, and what year?

In a matter of seconds, the giant screen was in place, a protective shield covering the town. Then everything around him was silent. Now, people in the street stopped and looked toward the sky, as if they awaited some sort of explanation. Even the cars stopped, and people stepped out onto the road. Nobody talked, nobody asked any questions.

Suddenly, there was a huge crash. It sounded like it came from far away, but also somehow close by. Jack turned around to locate the source of the sound. And he did not have to look for long. Suddenly, the sky was covered in fireballs making a right racket as they hammered against the shield. Jack held his hands over his ears and stared at the huge fireballs crashing into the shield every few seconds. He looked closer at the shield. It looked solid, but he was not convinced it would withstand the attack. There were big dents from all the fireballs.

Then the fireball attack slowly seemed to die out. Jack pulled himself together again and realised that he had crawled under a bench. Before he made it out from under the bench, he looked up from his hideaway and was startled to see a woman reaching out her hand to him. She was waving her hand around as if she wanted him to hold on to it. After a few moment's hesitation, he grabbed her hand and she dragged along the street. People were back to doing whatever they had been doing before the attack.

While the unknown woman rapidly led him down the street and into a small alleyway, Jack started noticing a metallic sound. Again, he looked to the sky. Along the inside of the shield, which was still in place, like a protective membrane, he saw shiny creatures move in on the damaged areas. More than anything, they looked like gigantic, mechanical spiders with really long legs. Were they actually repairing that strange shield?

Jack couldn't quite work out what was happening. He was hoping that the woman would be able to give him some answers. She was leading him away from the mechanical spiders along several streets lined with amazing villas to a safe place. He noticed sparks coming from above and objects falling to the ground. At the same time, he was trying hard to prevent the disk from falling out of his bag, which had been torn.

The woman stopped and turned around, and only now did Jack notice what she looked like. She had long, dark hair, it was almost black, and it fell below her shoulders. Green eyes lit up her sunburned face and the shapely eyebrows both framed and accentuated her eyes. She smiled and looked expectantly at him.

"Excuse me, but do you know which country and which year this is?"

She looked at him incomprehensively. Then she smiled again and said something which he didn't understand and walked away. The young woman turned her head and waved at him as she walked up a small flight of stone stairs leading up to a big house. The door closed behind her.

Jack looked around. He remembered this place, and continued down the pavement. Finally, he reached the place where he had landed face down on the grass. He went to the scrubs and was relieved to discover that it was indeed his landing site. He had no idea how long he had been gone.

Pulling out the disk, Jack noticed that it was dirty and damaged. He had banged and scratched it quite a few times, both as he fell to the ground and when he threw himself underneath the bench during that strange fireball attack. He dusted it with his hand as he looked around to see if anyone was watching him. And then he typed in the date and time and pressed the red button.

The journey back was also longer and noisier than before. As he alighted the time machine, he almost tripped and fell back into the machine. The room which had previously been the Professor's work space was now in what looked like ruins. Everything had been tossed around. Most of the books from the huge bookcase were spread across the floor and the furniture had been knocked over and flung into corners. Only then did Jack noticed the Professor who was standing in the middle of the mess, on top of one of the legs of the turned over desk.

The Professor held on to Jack with both hands, asking him if he was alright, but Jack had not quite come around yet. Then the Professor pulled up a chair and helped Jack sit down. The Professor started flicking through some papers, and when Jack finally came around, he staggered over to the Professor and sat down in front of him, on top of the knocked-over chest of drawers.

Finally, the Professor looked at him, but his eyes were vacant, and Jack wasn't sure whether he could even see him. Jack didn't know what to do other than ask him what had happened. There was a slight spark in the Professor's eyes as he seemed to waken from prolonged hibernation.

"I have no idea. I put the machine back together again, exactly as prescribed, so I don't know what went wrong."

Jack told him about the machine sending him to the future and not the past. The Professor stopped what he was doing and looked at Jack.

"But that's impossible."

He examined the machine and saw that it had been set for the past, not the future.

"You should probably go home and get some rest, then I'll find out what happened and try to sort out this chaos. Thank you so much for your help."

The Professor rose as he picked up another pile of papers from the floor. Jack also got up.

"But I would like to help you, as a way of thanking you for everything you've done for me. For choosing me to be the one who could travel back in time."

Jack did not wait for a reply, he just started picking up furniture and putting it back in its proper place. The Professor smiled vaguely and continued clearing stuff up. It was getting dark outside.

Jack would like to tell the Professor what he had experienced, but decided that it had probably better wait until the Professor found out what was wrong with the machine. On his way over to the door, the Professor said: "We must hope nobody heard that terrible noise from the machine."

Jack returned to his apartment utterly exhausted. But he couldn't sleep because of the thoughts in his head. After numerous attempts, he finally fell asleep.

The following day, Jack was too tired to carry out his routine, because he had only managed to get a few hours sleep. At work he tried to keep going and not fall asleep. Again, he managed to make it through the day practically without problems, and fortunately, the weekend was coming up, which meant he would be able to recuperate.

When he finished teaching, he couldn't help but try and find out more about the country he had visited the previous day. He searched for foreign languages online. For hours he sat there, checking out various websites, but none of them provided him with any evidence of having been in a foreign country. After several more hours, Jack felt his eyes were turning as square as the computer screen. He stood up. It felt like he had been sitting on his bottom for days.

Jack cycled over to the Professor's place to find out if he had discovered what had happened. He sincerely hoped that the Professor had gotten over yesterday's incident because then he might listen to what Jack had experienced during his last trip.

When he reached the front door, he had a sneaking suspicion that the house was being watched. He stopped and turned around, but like last time, he couldn't see anything. He knocked on the door and the Professor let him in.

"Hi, come on in, sit down," the Professor said. Jack could see that he was utterly exhausted. The place was back to normal, no signs of a bomb crater at all. They both sat on the lovely couch, resting both their legs and backs. Jack broke the silence, to tell the Professor about the strange things he had experienced during his journey to the future.

"I didn't go to the Jurassic period. I ended up in our world, but I don't know which country. Strange things happened that are not easily explained." Then Jack told the Professor about everything he had experienced, the cars pulled up by robotic arms, about the shield covering the town seconds before fireballs attacked and about the giant mechanical spiders repairing the shield.

The Professor was peacefully hunched over a pile of papers at his desk.

"I'm pleased to hear that you've not been frightened off by what happened yesterday."

He smiled, but somehow the smile never quite reached his eyes. Jack was dying to share more, and the Professor could tell. "I know you don't believe my story about what happened yesterday, but I know what I saw." Jack looked steadfastly at the Professor, hoping it would help him believe Jack's story. The Professor kept a straight face. Jack couldn't tell whether he was surprised or puzzled. After a long pause, he finally spoke.

"It can't possibly be true, Jack. I don't believe that it really happened. Are you sure, you haven't hit your head or something?"

The Professor looked a Jack with a silly expression and his face had seemingly come alive again. Jack was confused because the Professor seemed to deny Jack's experience. He wasn't sure what he should say. The Professor yawned and he looked tired.

"I'm sorry about what happened yesterday, but I've had quite a few problems with Dr Morris over the years, you see. I worked with him when I was younger, but then we fell out, and now he may be trying to get his hands on my secret inventions, which is why getting rid of the time machine may be important. But then again, it's not your battle to fight."

Jack couldn't keep his eyes open, and neither could the Professor. After a few hours, Jack woke up and wanted to get a drink. As he drank a glass of water, he glanced at the stairs down to the basement. Then he went down into the basement, and up to the time machine. He just stood and stared at it. He turned around to go back upstairs, but suddenly, he stopped and went to look at the red numbers. Jack frowned, something wasn't right. He moved closer and now he could see that the date that had been typed in was all wrong. He started counting the noughts and that was when he realised. He took a step back and dropped the glass of water. There was a nought too many.

Jack ran back upstairs, yelling the Professor's name. The Professor woke with a start and looked at Jack as he ran toward him. The Professor was frightened and believed that something very bad was about to happen. Jack pulled his arm and dragged him down to the time machine, while yelling: "I know what went wrong, I know what went wrong."

Jack showed the Professor the number with the extra nought. The Professor clasped his hands against his forehead and that was when Jack realised that something big had happened. Slowly, the smile evaporated. They were both in shock and neither of them knew how to deal with this huge discovery.

The Professor was standing rigid and didn't utter a sound. Then he moved away from the time machine which was usually in the corner. For a long time, he just stood and watched it, without moving a muscle.

"Oh, can it be true?"

The Professor's outburst had broken the silence and made Jack jump. The Professor ran to his desk and grabbed a ruler. Just as fast, he returned to the machine and held the ruler up against the small, oblong screen, which revealed which year the traveller was going to. He held it up to each nought as he spoke. He had to count and recount several times. Jack was behind him, looking over his shoulder.

"I can't believe it. Jack, you'll have to go back there again and find out more."

The Professor hurriedly scribbled down a few notes on a piece of paper.

"But, Professor, I don't get it. What do you mean, go back?"

At first, the Professor looked utterly uncomprehendingly at Jack, but then he realised that he hadn't shared his thoughts with Jack.

"Jack, I think we may have stumbled across something quite remarkable, something the world never knew. I actually believe that you went back, further back than the time of the dinosaurs."

Jack couldn't keep up with the Professor's torrent of words, but slowly, it dawned on him.

"Are you telling me that there were human's here, before the dinosaurs? That can't be true, because then we would have found traces of those humans."

The Professor gently shook his head.

"No, Jack, what I mean is that the world you have experienced could well be before the creation of our Earth. Before the Big Bang! Just like it happened with our world, there must have been another Big Bang, which brought another world into existence."

Now, Jack understood what the Professor was trying to tell him. And now, it was his turn to shake his head. Jack felt the butterflies in his stomach and nodded.

"Jack, you must tell me everything that happened on your last journey. I want to hear everything, down to even the smallest detail."

Telling the Professor everything took Jack a while. He tried to wring his brain firmly to make sure he included every detail. Once he finished, the Professor stared into space. The only thing Jack had left out was meeting that strange girl.

Jack was impatient, he wanted to know what the Professor had found out.

"Jack, I have to be honest, even if I'm not even sure about all of it myself. I seriously believe that you travelled back in time."

The Professor sounded so convinced of his own tale, but to Jack none of it made much sense. They had been travelling back in time, and the last place he had visited had been the present or perhaps even the future. They both sat down and the Professor said, "Can it really be true that there was another world before ours?" They spent quite a while absorbing this new concept. The Professor said that he would have to lie very low, until they found a way to handle these, quite shocking news.

"Go home, Jack, get some sleep," the Professor said. "I could do with a good night's sleep myself. Good night Jack, see you tomorrow, fresh as a fiddle, I hope."

The Professor walked Jack to the door. As the entered the street, he couldn't help but look both right and left. He had an odd, sneaking suspicion that someone was watching the house.

The following morning, Jack woke feeling on top of the world.

He had actually discovered something that he considered more interesting than the Jurassic period. It was only seven o'clock, and he didn't know what to do with himself. It was too early to head on over to the Professor's house, so he did his morning routine and cleaned the apartment.

Suddenly, the time flew by and Jack put on some clothes and set off. On his way over to the Professor, he kept looking around to see if anyone was following him. When he arrived, he could see that the Professor was also feeling great, and Jack was ever so keen to learn more about this other world. Once he had told him everything he had experienced, the Professor was also eager to go back in time and experience it for himself. But they decided that it was probably better if Jack went again and tried to find out more about the ways of that world, to prepare the Professor properly.

"Jack, are you ready to go back and find out more about that other world?"

They both hurried downstairs to the machine and as usual, Jack stepped inside. The Professor closed the door behind him and the usual humming commenced. But like the last time, Jack noticed that again, the journey seemed to take longer.

When everything went quiet and the shaking stopped, Jack slowly opened his eyes. He was in the middle of a dense forest. The only thing he could hear were the soft whispers in the tree-tops and the quiet chirping of birds.

At first, Jack wasn't sure what to do. He wasn't sure that he had arrived in the right period either. He had to try and find a way out of the forest before he would know for certain.

For a while, he walked around looking for a clearing, but without any luck. Then finally, he heard a noise that sounded like motorised vehicles. Jack sped up and walked in the direction of the sounds. He reached a busy road with cars hanging from the reversed conveyer belt. On the other side of the road, there was a quiet, residential neighbourhood.

As Jack got closer, he recognized the neighbourhood from his last visit. It seemed peaceful. Jack continued along the street until he reached the busy town centre where he had been, when the weird attack had taken place. He stopped and looked at the sky, but everything looked normal.

He continued down the street lined with shops that all had some kind of hologram above their entrance. He was not quite sure whether he was in exactly the same spot as last time, because it was a bit darker now, but it appeared to be the same strange language written on the signs above the shops.

Having wondered around for a while, soaking up all the new impressions, he noticed that people were wearing a kind of headset and talking on their phones. Jack was not impressed, but then he noticed others talking on the phone by way of some kind of hologram that seemed to emerge from their headset. Each time they spoke, the image changed. Jack could only guess that it was connected to the Internet, and that people used their voices to go online and browse for information, because they held nothing in their hands.

He walked pass the harbour and noticed the large freight and cruise ships, which were much bigger than the ones he had seen in his own world. They were not that much taller, but they were much broader, at least double the width of the ones in his world. It looked like two ships had been merged, but only at the top, and the passengers emerged from the middle of the ship. It looked like a catamaran, only much bigger.

Next to the harbour there was what looked like an airport, and the airplanes were constructed the same way, as if two airplanes had been merged. He looked at his watch and was surprised to discover that he had been wandering around for five hours. Only now did he noticed that the shadows were getting longer, a sure sign that the sun was setting in the horizon.

Jack started backtracking, hoping that he would be able to remember the way back. Once he left the town centre and was heading toward the forest, he caught a glimpse of the mystical woman who had helped him to safety during his last visit. And so, he turned down the road she was on.

Suddenly, everything turned quite dark. The shadows from the trees didn't help. Then he heard voices further ahead and the sound of feet on the ground. Jack froze and listened. He couldn't work out how far away they were. He hunched over and sneaked forward.

Now, he saw lights flashing ahead of him. And then suddenly, he felt a hand squeezing his shoulder hard from behind. He was taken completely by surprise and almost lost his balance, falling backwards. He managed to straighten himself up, though, and quickly swung around. In the dim light, he couldn't see the face of the other person, now standing in front of him, but he had no doubts.

The loose hair cascading over the marked shoulders, blowing gently in the soft wind. It was the woman, who had helped him get away during his last visit. She started speaking in the language that Jack understood absolutely nothing of, so instead, he tried to communicate using signs and body language. She smiled and laughed a little and then moved on.

Jack had seen enough for one day, and now he really wanted to get back to the forest, where it would be safe to take out the disk without anyone watching. However, he couldn't get the beautiful woman out his head and he couldn't help smiling.

When Jack returned to his own world, he looked like someone who was slightly intoxicated, a little dizzy, yet smiling broadly. The Professor spoke to him straight away, eager to find out about everything Jack had experienced.

"It was such a wonderful experience. The people look like us, behave like us and think like us. They have everything we have, except they appear to be much more developed." And then there was the woman, the most beautiful woman he had ever laid eyes on. She was flawless, her hair, eyes, lips and nose, everything was simply perfect.

After talking to the Professor for hours, Jack went home, pulling his bike, not cycling. He wanted to savour the last few hours of a perfect day.

When he arrived home, he threw himself on the bed and stared at the ceiling. He conjured up her image and couldn't get her out of his head. He had never felt this way about anybody, and he didn't even know her name. Was that what they called love at first sight? Or rather second sight? Jack turned over on his side and fell asleep.

The next day, he had to prepare for spending the day with his family, and so he got dressed while humming. Once, he was dressed, he got in his car and drove to his parents' house. On arrival, he received the usual warm welcome and great food all wrapped in a lovely atmosphere.

After eating, they all just sat around chitchatting. Everyone could tell that Jack was in a good mood.

"I hope you've sorted that stuff out you talked about last time," his mother said. Jack confirmed and said that he had, and even more than that.

"That happy face can only mean one thing: Jack's met a woman!" his brother James shouted. "It's the same smile I had on my face when I met my wife."

Jack blushed and said that they shouldn't get their hopes up, because he and the girl hadn't talked much.

"Tell me what you talked about," James said. "Then I'll tell you what it means, because I'm an expert on women."

They all laughed, and Jack said that they had communicated by way of body language rather than spoken language.

"But shouldn't we wait? We can talk more about her when I've spoken to her some more. Then we can see what develops from that."

It had been a lovely day, and now it was time to go home, so they all got in their cars and drove home. When Jack arrived home, Dr Morris appeared again, out of the blue, giving Jack a shock.

"What can I do for you, Dr Morris?"

"The other day, I heard a noise coming from the Professor's house, and I'll do everything in my power to find out if anything happened. Perhaps he dropped something big. I'm keeping my eye on you two." As he was about to leave, Jack grabbed his arm and said that this was his second warning. Dr Morris had better stay away from them or he would tell the police.

Then Jack went up to his apartment and locked the door. He had no time to think about Dr Morris, because he had papers to mark.

The next day, he went to see the Professor in his office, he wanted to tell him about Dr Morris waiting outside his front door when he arrived home last night. And how he had said that he had heard noises coming from the Professor's house.

"Nothing to worry about, Jack. I spent all day Sunday adding an extra layer of insulation and updating my security systems. However, now I'm also eager to visit that other world, and neither Dr Morris nor anyone else is going to stop me from doing just that. I have some papers to finish marking, but come by after work, and we will talk more."

After work, Jack went to the Professor's house. He opened the door before Jack even rang the bell, and as Jack entered, he noticed things that had not been there before. The Professor showed him the camera, situated above the window, and pointing to the road where a sensor had been fastened to the doors and windows.

Then they went down into the basement, where the Professor showed Jack the extra layer of insulation he had added. Then the Professor went back upstairs again, and continued working on whatever it was he was doing.

He continued talking about what they should do, and how they should handle Dr Morris. They agreed that the next time he showed up at Jack's place, the Professor would call the police and get rid of him once and for all.

It was getting late, and Jack realised that he would not be visiting the other world today. So, he grabbed his coat, jumped on his bike and headed home. Cycling home and all through the entire evening, he couldn't stop thinking about the woman and how much he looked forward to seeing her again.

The next day was a quiet day, he concentrated on his work even if it was proving a little difficult, because his thoughts kept wandering to the other world, and the beautiful woman in particular. After work, he went to the Professor's house to find out if there were any news.

As soon as the Professor let Jack inside the house, he pulled him toward a TV-screen showing what was happening on the street. The Professor pointed to the screen and told Jack that a car with a man inside it had been parked there ever since he got home. You couldn't see who was sitting in the car, so Jack would have to crawl out of the basement window with a pair of binoculars and then get as close to the car as possible to find out who it was.

A few minutes later, Jack returned and told the Professor that it was Dr Morris. The Professor immediately called the police, telling them that a man, possibly a paedophile was sitting in a black Ford outside 1594, Vincent Road.

Shortly after, the police arrived and Jack and the Professor could see that they started asking Dr Morris questions. He became very aggressive and uncooperative, so the policemen arrested him and drove him to the police station.

Immediately after, Jack and the Professor went down into the basement to get the time machine up and running. And as soon as it was ready, the Professor got in and travelled back to that other world. Jack was disappointed that he would only be able to go once the Professor returned. He was afraid that he would not make it there today either.

However, the Professor quickly returned and said that he had experienced as much as he could cope with for one day. Jack was so surprised and said, "But you've only been gone a few minutes."

"It's a time machine, Jack. I can stay in the past for several days and come back to the present when I want to."

Jack was a little embarrassed at not having figured that out by himself, but he was excited because it meant that he might make it to the other world today after all. Only, the Professor continued talking about everything he had experienced and how fascinating it had been.

Jack realised that he would be going nowhere today, but if he waited until Friday, he would have so much more time to experience the other world, without having to think about having to get up for work the following day.

For the next two days, he tried to concentrate only on work, leaving the weekend free from chores of any kind so he could visit the other world. This was why he never went to see the Professor but only focused on work.

When Friday arrived, he was ready to leave as soon as he finished teaching at the university, and shortly after, he was outside the Professor's door, ready to travel to the other world. Not many words were exchanged between the Professor and Jack, because the Professor sensed that Jack was eager to get going.

He slapped Jack's shoulder and said: "Let's get moving then." And before he knew it, Jack was back in that other world, where he started searching for the woman right away. Having wandered up and down the street, where they first met, for a while, he suddenly saw her. He felt the butterflies in his stomach, much like a young child at Christmas.

He tried to talk to her, but she held a finger to her mouth and started walking in the direction Jack had just arrived from. Without a second thought, Jack followed her. Suddenly, they could hear shouting voices behind them. It was obviously a group of people who had heard them. The young woman darted down various streets at great speed. Jack could barely keep up and felt clumsy as he moved through this unfamiliar landscape.

The voices increased in strength and figuring out how close they were was not easy. It occurred to Jack that if he was caught or killed in this world, the future may well turn out completely differently.

Finally, they reached the end of the street and turned onto a road that Jack recognized. He only realised that he had stopped when the young woman grabbed his hand and pulled him along.

The foreign woman led him to the same building where she had left him the first time. Putting in quite an effort, they made it to the top floor. Jack tried to hide how out of breath he was, having climbed the numerous steep stairs, but it merely caused a stinging sensation in his side.

Jack collapsed on a white sofa, and after a short while he had gathered enough strength to explore the room further. It was a small room, but the atmosphere was lovely with the dark windows and dim lights. He couldn't see the woman, who had brought him here, but then she entered the room.

Only now did Jack notice what his saviour or kidnapper looked like. She was tall and slender, with very long legs. Her auburn hair was long and straight. Her face had fine features and her skin was light. She walked around opening and closing cupboards and drawers, tidying lots of papers and she paid Jack no attention whatsoever.

Jack felt tired and exhausted and closed his eyes, but he couldn't settle his thoughts. Through his half-closed eyes, he could see that the woman had stopped moving and was examining him attentively. She went to the sink and filled a glass with water. She almost hovered across the floor and handed Jack the glass.

"Drink all of it, it'll help."

Without thinking about it, Jack gulped the water down. He fell back on the sofa and felt a sleepiness envelop his body and his head. He sighed and fell into a dreamless sleep.

When he woke up, he saw an elderly gentleman talking to the woman. He looked around the room and tried to locate his rucksack with the disk. Suddenly, the man and woman noticed him and they both walked over. They held what looked like a drawing of planet Earth, but it looked different from the maps Jack was familiar with.

The elderly man pointed to the map and grabbed Jack's hand firmly as he tried to make Jack point to the place where he was from. But Jack was petrified and didn't utter a word. The started talking to the woman in the language Jack didn't understand. Judging by their tone of voice, they were not discussing pleasant matters.

Then the elderly man stormed out, slamming the door shut behind him. The woman sat down next to Jack with a map of the world in her hand and said something, only, he did not understand what she was trying to say. He looked for his rucksack and placed his hand gently on top of hers as if to indicate that his intentions were peaceful. Then he picked up something to write with and started drawing a new world map. He tried to explain, using signs and gesticulations, that he was not of this world.

The woman did not understand what Jack was trying to say and so he began drawing the time machine according to his memory, and again, he tried to explain step by step, how he had ended up here.

After a while, the woman appeared to finally understand and she jumped up clasping her hands in front of her mouth in shock. Jack also stood up, placing his arms around the shocked woman. He told her that he would like to see her again, still only using signs and gesticulations. She, however, was in despair and not sure what to do with herself. Jack searched the room for his rucksack and when he saw it, he ran to get it in order to check if the disk was still there. It was! Then Jacked checked it to see if anyone else had touched it or accidentally destroyed it. It looked fine. Then Jack went back to the woman and held her close as he said: "I'll see you again soon." Then he left.

On his way back to the forest, he looked over his shoulder to check if he was being followed, only he never noticed that the woman was right behind him. When he arrived at the forest, he took out the disk, typed in date and time and then disappeared. The woman was able to see with her own eyes that everything he had told her was true.

When Jack returned to his own time, he failed to mention to the Professor what had happened in the woman's apartment. He also failed to mention the elderly, angry man. He only told the Professor what had happened before he met the woman.

Jack and the Professor spent all day and evening talking about the other world; this magnificent discovery they had made. It was getting late and Jack was ready to head home. But before he left, he wanted to make sure that he would be able to go back to the other world again the following day.

He woke early the next day, too early to go see the Professor, so instead, he went to the shooting range to pass the time. At 12 o'clock Noon, Jack went to the Professor's house, where the Professor had everything ready so that Jack could simply head straight for the time machine.

Within no time at all, he was back in the clearing, which he recognised. He got up on his feet and walked toward the building in which the woman lived. He managed to get inside the building and up to her apartment where he knocked on the door. When she opened, she was not sure what to do, but Jack smiled so broadly at seeing her again that she let him in.

He entered the apartment and sat on the sofa. He patted the cushion next to him, signalling that she should come over and sit down next to him. The woman sat down, placed her hands on her knees and lowered her head.

Jack placed a finger under her jaw and lifted her head and then he kissed her on the mouth. He had not considered whether it was the proper thing to do, but as she did not kiss him back, he opened his eyes and looked into her beautiful blue eyes.

For a few moments they just sat there, looking at each other, slowly moving closer and eventually they started kissing each other, intimately. And then they talked for a very long time, using only signs and body language.

Jack discovered that her name was Reynora Treynora and she explained where the fire balls came from. It turned out that her country was at war with another country and sometimes they fired shots at each other. Which was also why they had to run away from the people who had been following them, because if Jack did not speak their language, they might want to hurt and possibly even kill him.

Jack noticed that none of her electric appliances were plugged in, yet they were switched on. He started wondering where the electricity came from. The woman laughed and explained that they had wireless electricity, which at first, Jack didn't understand. Eventually, he realised that there was only one powerplant, which supplied everyone with wireless electricity.

Having talked for hours, they went for a walk. Reynora's headphone, which was also a telephon,e rang. A hologram emerged in front of her face. He had seen it before, only not right up close, and he was fascinated. He could tell that it was her father, and he managed to find out that her father was coming to meet them.

When he arrived, her father did not look pleased. But after a while, it was clear that he was more relaxed. Then all three of them went for a walk. They tried to communicate using signs. Reynora tried to tell Jack that she had told her father everything about him because her father was the only family she had left and they kept no secrets from each other.

Suddenly, there was huge bang. It came from above and they all looked up. A huge aeroplane was on fire and speeding towards the ground very rapidly. The shield re-emerged and covered the town.

Jack noticed that the plane was dissolving, not because of the flames, but it looked like it was shedding the burning bits until only the cabin was left. Some sort of parachute opened up and eased the cabin down toward the ground. A few moments before impact, some sort of airbag appeared underneath the cabin, which would probably secure a soft landing, Jack thought to himself.

Just when everyone believed that the worst was over and the survivors were getting help, they heard a seeping noise and they all looked up. Suddenly, the sky was filled with fire balls impacting the protective shield in the same spots that the plane had damaged it, in other words, in its weak spots. Which made the protective shield even weaker.

Jack grabbed hold of Reynora and her father and tried to get them away from the danger, before the shield collapsed. But Reynora's father wrenched himself free of Jack's grip and went back to help the survivors. A fire ball hit the shield in what to Jack appeared to be slow motion and penetrated the shield.

There was a huge explosion and many people were knocked over like they were nothing but ragdolls. Reynora tried to get to her father, but Jack held her back. When it was over, they wanted to find out if he had been hurt, but the police and rescue teams would not let them through at first. However, when Reynora saw her father lying lifeless on the ground, surrounded by people trying to help him, nothing could hold her back. With tears streaming from her eyes, she ran to him, and at the sound of her voice, her father opened his eyes slowly and said something Jack did not understand. He guessed that the father told his daughter that he loved her. Reynora held his hands and burst out crying, while taking to her father. And then he passed away.

All Jack could do was hold her tight and try to comfort her as best he could. When it was all over, and the rescue teams were packing up, Jack brought Reynora back to her apartment. Jack did everything he could to comfort her, when suddenly, she jumped up, fetched a piece of paper and started drawing something. She was trying to explain to Jack that they could use his devise to go back in time and rescue her father.

It was not easy, but Jack tried to explain to her that you should not change the past. All he could do was tell her that he would try to go back to his own time and try to find out if there was anything he could do for her.

Jack was not sure whether or not she understood what he was trying to tell her. And he was not happy about leaving her behind, but he had to go back if he was to find out if there was anything he could do to help her.

When Jack arrived back in his own time, he told the Professor exactly what had happened, and he asked the Professor if he believed that there was anything they could do to help the woman?

The Professor had to think about it. He told Jack that he was working on a new disk, which would allow both of them to travel to the past and experience it together. Only now, he would have to think about what Jack had told him.

Jack went home, but he couldn't sleep. He tried to come up with some way of helping Reynora and her father.

The following morning, he called his parents to cancel family lunch, because he would rather spend time with the Professor, to see if they could find a way of helping Reynora.

When he arrived at the Professor's, the Professor was surprised to see him so early, because he thought that Jack was going to a family lunch. And then it dawned on him, just how much Reynora meant to Jack.

They sat down and tried to come up with a way to help her father without creating utter chaos in the other world. After many hours, they came up with a solution: Jack would go back to their world, on the day before the incident, and if he could convince the father to come back to their world and thus vanish from his own world, it might work.

Only, Jack would have to go there again, to see Reynora and tell her about this idea. And so, the Professor started the machine and Jack prepared himself for yet another time travel.

Soon, he was back in that other world. Jack went straight to Reynora's apartment to tell her about their plan. But when he arrived, she wasn't there. He had to wait outside until she came home. He couldn't help thinking about whether anything had happened to her, if she had possibly injured herself.

After a while, Reynora came home and Jack ran to her and gave her a hug. Then they entered her apartment and Jack tried to explain what they considered to be the best plan.

Reynora was not happy about her father leaving, but on the other hand, she was very pleased that this way, he might survive. They hugged and kissed passionately for a while. And then Jack pulled back her hair, stared into her beautiful eyes and suggested that both her and her father should come back to his world.

Reynora was quiet for a moment, she was not sure what to say. She thought long and hard about everything that was going on in her life right now, and how life without her father would be terribly sad. They talked for a few hours about what would be the best thing to do. But then Jack had to get himself ready to go back to his own world. Before leaving, he kissed her. He couldn't get enough of her.

Jack returned to his own world and immediately told the Professor about the decision they had made. The Professor was not entirely convinced though, afraid that their plan might have an effect on that other world.

Jack argued that it didn't matter what happened in that other world, because it no longer existed. But then the Professor argued that their world was dependent on that world. And if that other world was affected, there was no way of knowing how it would impact this world.

"I need to think some more on it, and furthermore, I haven't completed the other disk yet."

Jack asked if there was anything he could do to help, but the Professor would rather work alone. It was not terribly late yet, and so Jack decide that he would go see his family anyway. He would rather spend half a day with them than not see them at all. The Professor lent him his car, so he wouldn't have to cycle home to get his own car.

Jack's family were surprised, but happy to see him. They were still eating and Jack joined them. He enjoyed his mother's lovely food. Afterwards, they sat in the garden, and everyone was excited to know more about the new love in Jack's life.

Jack, however, would only reveal that it was more complicated than he had thought at first. Only time would show what would happen.

Evening descended and everyone got ready to go home. Except Jack. He stayed because he wanted to talk to his father. He hoped that his father would be able to help him with his problem. He asked his father to sit down, because the story he was about to hear would knock him off his feet. He also made his father promise that he would not tell anyone else about any of it.

His father became anxious and prepared himself for the worst. Jack told him everything he had been through over the last few weeks. Jack's father slumped farther and farther back in his chair while rubbing his eyes. He said that he hoped Jack was not having him on. Only, when he looked at the expression on Jack's face, he knew that Jack was being quite serious.

The father rose from his chair and started pacing, hands clasped behind his back. Jack was not sure what he expected his father to say, and Jack's father did not know what to say, other than agreeing with what the Professor said because it made sense that what happened in that other world would have an effect on this world. Unless Reynora's father was "dead". "Then you could bring him back to our world."

Jack asked his father what he meant by "dead"? And his father replied that he remembered something about how people could be injected with something that would make them appear to be dead for half an hour or so, and then it would be possible to resuscitate them. Then again, it was something he had only seen and heard about on the television. He was not sure whether it was true. His father simply had to agree that it was a very difficult decision to have to make. He argued that Jack should follow his heart. Only he could decide what would be the right thing to do.

Jack put on his coat and said goodbye to his father and mother. Then he drove to the Professor's where he would leave the car. When he arrived there, he told the Professor about his father's suggestion, without revealing that it was his father's suggestion.

However, the Professor refused to even contemplate the thought, because it was simply not possible. Reynora's father would have to go to hospital, where they would keep him in cold storage until someone could check up on him and that would take a lot longer than half an hour.

"And if you were able to remove him from the scene of the accident within half an hour, you wouldn't have the resources to resuscitate him."

Jack didn't know what to say or do. It was getting late and so he decided to cycle home and get some sleep. After all, he had to go to work the next day.

When the alarm went off, Jack's body felt completely wrecked and he wanted to call in sick. Only, that was not really an option as he was newly employed and so he had to grind his teeth and find a way of getting through the day.

For lunch, he met up with the Professor. He wanted to know if the Professor had come up with a plan. But as always, the Professor did not want to discuss any of it at the university. Jack would have to wait until the evening.

When the last lesson was successfully completed, he rushed over to the Professor's house. However, when he arrived, he noticed an unfamiliar car parked in the driveway.

Jack slowly approached the front door, he was not sure what was going on. Suddenly, the door opened and two men in cheap suits came out, heading straight for the car. Jack was anxious to know who they were and what they had wanted with the Professor, who waved at them as they drove off.

As soon as they were out of sight, the Professor and Jack went back into the house and the Professor revealed that the two men were from the CIA, they had come to check up on his work on the time machine. After all, they had not granted him permission to continue working on it, once the programme had been discontinued. Apparently, Dr Morris had told them about his suspicions when he was arrested.

"Fortunately, though, they only asked questions, and I told them that Dr Morris had turned a little crazy after the project was closed down, which kept them out of the basement."

They sat down and Jack wondered what the Professor's next move would be, because he could tell that it was all getting a little too much for the elderly man. And then the Professor said what Jack had feared the most:

"We must get rid of the time machine."

Jack's heart dropped and he tried to convince the Professor that he simply could not abandon the greatest achievement of his life just because a couple of guys from the CIA started asking questions.

"It's routine, someone says something and they have to investigate. But now that they've been here, they won't come back."

Naturally, the Professor was not happy about dismantling his life's work and so he went into the basement to continue working on the new disk. Jack followed him down there, eager to find out what would happen to Reynora's father. The Professor was quiet for a while and then he said that they would have to see what happened. Whether or not the world would change if they brought him back to this world. However, Jack had to promise the Professor that if there was even the slightest change, they would return him immediately.

Jack could not wait to see Reynora again, to tell her the good news, but he didn't like having to ask the Professor for permission. He would rather that the Professor suggested it himself, because he didn't want to come across as pushy. The Professor picked up on Jack's eagerness to see Reynora again and started up the time machine. Before long, Jack was back in the other world.

When Reynora opened her front door, she could tell that Jack had good news. Because why else would he be smiling? It had to be because he had good news to share. Jack told her everything and then it was time for him to go back again. They stood outside the door for a very long time, kissing. Jack could not get enough of his woman. But he had no other option, he had to get back to his world.

Upon his return, he could see that the Professor was busy completing the second disk. As Jack came around, the Professor asked if everything was okay in the other world. Jack told him how happy Reynora was because they had decided to help her and her father.

Jack and the Professor spent all evening making plans, deciding on what to do and how. Before Jack went back home, the Professor said that if all went well, he expected to have the second disk finished by the following day. Jack was exhausted from his travels, so he went straight home and fell asleep.

After the last lesson, he cycled to the Professor's house as they had agreed. The Professor wanted to join Jack on a time travelling trip, to make sure the disk worked properly before Jack went on his own. That would also give them a chance to experience the other world together. What the Professor was most excited about was meeting the woman who clearly had stolen Jack's heart.

However, the machine only had room for one, so they would have to travel separately. Jack stepped into the machine first and after only a few moments, he was gone. After a few minutes, they were both in the other world. They shared their previous experiences.

Before long, they were both in front of Reynora's apartment. She opened the door and was surprised to see the two of them. But instantly, she also understood that she would very likely get to see her father again soon. She hugged and kissed Jack and then she also gave the Professor a big hug.

As they stepped into the living room, the Professor told Jack that he completely understood why he had fallen in love with her. "She is gorgeous!" He looked around the apartment, fascinated by the wireless electricity which supplied not only her apartment but the entire town.

Then all three of them sat down on the sofa. They discussed what would happen and when. The Professor explained that when they were convinced that the second disk was working, they could go back to their own world and then Jack would have to go back again. Only the main machine could decide which time period you travelled to.

Having planned everything down to the tiniest detail, Jack and the Professor went back to their own world. And when they arrived, the Professor said that he believed Friday would be the best day for Jack to go back because they were quite exhausted right now, both of them.

"And we have day jobs, you know. Plus, Friday is not long off, only a couple of days."

Speak for youself, Jack thought to himself.

When he arrived back home, Dr Morris was waiting for him. He was the last person Jack wanted to see or talk to, so he immediately fished out his mobile phone to call the police. But Dr Morris grabbed his hand before he was able to lift the phone to his ear. He told Jack that he was well aware of what was going on and he would not give in until he discovered the truth. And then he left.

That was the one thing Jack did not want to hear. Once again, Dr Morris had placed Jack in a dilemma, should he tell the Professor or not? Jack could not sleep because of what Dr Morris had said. He contemplated what to say to the Professor and not least how the Professor would react.

Most of all, though, he thought of Reynora. And whether he would ever get to see her again. What if he had to break the promise he had made about her father?

The following day, Jack was far from his best, and to top it all off, Mrs Trisseltoft wanted to see him in her office. It was not one of her good days. At first, she looked through some papers with students' grades. It did not look good. Jack's students were losing interest in his subject and he had to do something or they would have to close it down and Jack would be without a job. He had to find a way of getting the students interested again.

The first thing he did was talk about planet Earth. How it had evolved and what came before the Big Bang. The rest of the week, Jack spoke of little else, and he set them a couple of assignments that would hopefully reignite their interest in the Jurassic period. And it actually made the time pass more rapidly.

As Friday arrived, Jack had no time to waste. He jumped on his bike and went to see the Professor, who had everything ready. But before they went to the other world on the day that Reynora's father died, they would first have to go and get her, because she was the only one, who would be able to explain to her father what was about to happen. It would be a long day with much travelling back and forth, but it was the only way to get all of them safely back to Jack's world.

They went to get Reynora. Then she and Jack returned, and once she had settled in at the Professor's house, Jack went back to get the Professor. Then Jack and Reynora would go back together. They would time it so that they would be there an hour before her father was killed. After a long chat with her father, Reynora managed to persuade him to go back with Jack, and while the Professor took care of Reynora's father, Jack went back to get her.

However, after the third trip, the machine was getting overheated and it started shaking. The Professor had not taken this into account, so he had to work fast to fix it. Meanwhile, Jack and Reynora could not understand why they were unable to return. And they were getting frightened that something had gone wrong. What Jack feared more than anything was involvement from Dr Morris. The only thing they could do was return to Reynora's apartment and then try again later.

Back in the Professor's house, Reynora's father came around. And looking around the room, he suddenly noticed the Professor. He tried to explain what was wrong, but Reynora's father misunderstood and thought that they were out to hurt his daughter.

Suddenly, he attacked the Professor and they ended up rolling around on the floor. Eventually, the Professor managed to overpower him. Then he tried to explain to Reynora's father that they were in fact only trying to help them both. That calmed Reynora's father down considerably and the Professor could get back to work on the machine. After a while, Reynora's father rose from the chair and offered to help. Finally, they made it work again, but they were unable to reach Jack and Reynora to let them know that it was working, so all they could do was wait for them to show up.

Jack tried to get the disk to reconnect with the time machine and after several attempts he succeeded. Jack sent Reynora first, and when the disk was ready to go again, he hurried back before something else went wrong. Now, they were all safely back in Jack's world.

It had taken Reynora a while to get there, but once she saw her father's smiling face, she almost jumped into the air from joy, as she realised that their plan had worked. However, they were all exhausted.

It was getting dark, and Reynora was out on the terrace, leaning against the door, watching the sun set. Jack came up from behind and held her tightly. He kissed her shoulder. Reynora leaned her head back against Jack's shoulder and closed her eyes to enjoy this perfect moment.

The Professor was eagerly listening to the stories Reynora's father was telling him. They laughed and had a great time. However, as the evening wore on, Jack wanted to spend some time alone with Reynora. Reynora agreed and they borrowed the Professor's car. That would give them some time at Jack's place, before she would have to go back again.

Jack had butterflies in his stomach, it was a lovely feeling and everything seemed just right. He had never felt that way about a woman before. Jack put on some romantic music and made passionate love to Reynora.

In the morning, the Professor phoned him to remind him that her father missed her, and that he and his time machine were feeling a bit left out. Jack said that they were on their way and that they would bring breakfast.

"Lunch, more like," the Professor said.

They spent all day Saturday showing Reynora and her father the town. They had ice cream because the weather was still warm. But as evening approached, it was time for Reynora to go back, because she had obligations in her world as well.

Jack and Reynora were not happy about the prospect of leaving each other, but she had to go, and so the Professor sent Jack and Reynora back in order that Jack could bring back the disk.

Jack had no intention of returning straight away, though. He wanted to make the most of the time he had with Reynora, and so he stayed until she was fast asleep.

Upon his return, he felt empty and alone. It was as if a part of him was missing. But he also noticed how well the Professor and Reynora's father got on, they seemingly had so much in common, and then he realised that as long as her father was here, he would always have Reynora in his life. The three men spent the entire evening talking.

Eventually, Jack had to head home, as he was seeing his family the next day. He was a little worried about how his father would react because of what they had talked about last week. But he needn't have been. His father was his usual self.

After dinner though, when they were all sitting around chatting, Jack's father implied that he would like a quiet word with Jack. They went into the living room and Jack's father asked him what decision he had finally made. Jack was not sure how much he should reveal, as he didn't want his father to worry more than he already did. After all, he was an elderly gentleman and already a bit stressed. Which was why he decided to tell him that everything had worked out just fine. The world had not change one little bit. He should stop worrying. Jack's father was so relieved to hear it and had nothing more to say on the matter. Then they joined the others.

"Have you been talking to Dad about the wedding?" James asked as soon as he saw Jack. "When do we get to meet this mystery woman?"

"Soon," Jack said. "Very soon."

On his way back, Jack decided to look in on the Professor, to check up on Reynora's father. He even entertained the idea that the Professor had gone back to the other world to fetch Reynora, but when the Professor let him in, there were no signs of her there. They all talked for a while, but as Jack was getting bored with their chitchat he decided to go home instead.

Just as he was heading out of the front door, two men approached, introducing themselves as CIA agents. They wanted to know how much Jack new about the Professor and whether or not he was secretly working on anything.

Jack told them that he knew nothing, except that the man was a Professor at the university. They asked him lots of question, but Jack insisted that he only knew him as a colleague. Then they two agents got back in their car and drove off.

When he got home, he rubbed his face hard as he contemplated what he had gotten himself mixed up in. It would soon have to stop, or there would be consequences. Jack's life was turning into hell.

The next day, he went to see the Professor to tell him what was going on. How strange people looked him up all the time, asking questions. Maybe their luck was running out and it would all go wrong at some point. The Professor agreed.

"Perhaps we simply have to stop while the going is still good? But we have to go on one last journey to let Reynora know, before we destroy the machine."

Jack went to see the Professor after work, he was ready to go back, they had no time to waste. They explained what they were about to do to Reynora's father and perhaps he should consider asking Reynora to join them here in their world for ever, because that would be the only way they could stay together.

However, Reynora's father was not keen on that idea and he tried to persuade them to reconsider, before they burnt the bridge linking their two worlds. Perhaps, the Professor could dismantle the machine and store the various parts in different places. The Professor would not promise anything.

First and foremost, they had to pick up Reynora so they could work something out together. The Professor had already prepared the time machine, and there was no time to waste, so Jack hurried along to the other world.

Reynora was very pleased to see him and she gave him a huge hug. But she could sense that all was not well, and so she took a step back. She could tell from his face that he was not as happy as he usually was. She asked him what was wrong. Jack wouldn't say much, only that they had to get to his world in a hurry. He and the Professor would explain everything once they were there. The he set the timer on her disk first, then on his own, and before long, both of them were back in the Professor's basement. Reynora's father did most of the talking, because it was easier and faster. Meanwhile, the Professor set about dismantling the machine. Reynora did not understand what was going on, and she broke down in tears. Jack tried to comfort her. And she tried to explain to him that she also had a life back in her world, she had a job and her own apartment. Jack tried to explain that this world also contained everything she would ever need. She had him and her father, and "We can always get you a job and an apartment."

After much talking and many tears, the Professor wanted Jack's help with lifting something, and so he went to assist him. Reynora and her father went out on the terrace. Her father tried to comfort her. Jack stopped and looked back at Reynora, realising just how happy he was that she was in his life. Then he continued down stairs.

They spent the entire evening dismantling the time machine. They tried to figure out what to do with all the parts. They decided that some could be stored at Jack's parents', at Jack's place and in his office at the university, while the rest would have to remain here.

They were all tired and exhausted. Jack took Reynora's hand and told her they would go back to his place to get some sleep. The Professor lent them his car. Jack could drop off Reynora the next morning and then he and the Professor could drive to work together.

As the alarm went off the next morning, Jack turned over in his bed to see if it had all been a dream. But when he saw Reynora there, his face lit up in a big smile. He cuddled up to her before getting out of bed to do his morning routine. Then Jack drove to the Professor's. Reynora got out and the Professor in, and they drove off heading for the university.

It turned into a great day at work. He was beginning to sus out how to get the students interested in his subject, he managed to get them to see how exciting it actually was.

After work, he and the Professor went to look at cars. Now that he had a woman in his life a bike was no longer sufficient and the old scrap heap that he drove around in was not quite the thing either.

Jack had dreamt of being able to buy a new car and now that he had a steady job, it was time to invest. He got a good price, and in a few days, he would be able to pick it up from the dealer. Then they went back to the Professor's house. They were looking forward to spending time with Reynora and her father.

When they entered the house, a stranger was sitting on the sofa with two large men behind him. Reynora and her father were nowhere to be seen. Jack and the Professor were speechless. At the same time, they heard noises coming from the basement. Jack went to see what was going on, but one of the big guys stepped out from behind the sofa and stopped him.

"Sit down," said the man sitting on the sofa.

Jack had lots of questions, but somehow the words stuck in his throat. He fumbled with the sofa's cushions but finally, he managed to say: "Who are you, and what do you want?"

The man spoke with a Russian accent and he told them that he knew all about them. He had heard that the Professor had a time machine. And he would very much like to get his hands on it. Jack froze and was terribly upset. All he could say was that he knew nothing about it and what on earth made them think that he had such a thing? The Russian man said: "A little bird told me that Dr Morris told the police about you and a time machine." They had been to see Dr Morris and after some time and a little torture, he had admitted that he had told the CIA about the Professor and that he was very possibly building a time machine.

"And as you can see, we are connected so don't make the mistake of thinking that we are stupid. Just tell us what we want to hear."

The Professor was quiet, he never said anything. At the same time, Jack realised that perhaps one of these men were the reason the project the Professor had worked on for the CIA was discontinued. Just then, one of the men returned from the basement. Seeing him, the Professor exclaimed "Fatkov!"

Jack asked the Professor if he knew the man, and he said, "Yes, we used to work together back in the day." Jack was very pleased that they had decided to dismantle the machine before these men showed up. Finally, the Professor decided to say something.

"It was all just something Dr Morris imagined. That I would continue the work Fatkov and I had carried out after project was discontinued." None of the men in the room looked convinced, but Jack was more worried about Reynora and her father and so he got up from his chair and headed for the basement. Only, he was stopped. Jack grabbed the hand of the man who stopped him.

The two men standing behind the man on the sofa, their boss, pulled out their weapons, which made the Professor jump out of his chair and tell everybody to calm down, because there was nothing for them here. "I'm afraid you've been misinformed."

Jack pushed the man's hand away. The boss rose from the sofa and told them that he did not believe a single word of what they were saying and that only time would tell who was right and who was wrong. Then he jerked his head sideways, signalling that they were leaving.

Once they left, Jack hurried down into the basement to see if Reynora and her father were all right. Fortunately, they had managed to hide in the secret room that the Professor had built for the time machine.

Reynora was quite shaken and frightened, but Jack held her and told her that everything was okay. Having made sure that they were alright, he got in his car. But before he could leave, the Professor asked him where he was going. Jack told him that he wanted to get this over and done with once and for all. He was going to see Dr Morris. On his way there, he stopped at his own apartment and picked up a gun. Jack was furious, he had had enough.

When he reached Dr Morris, he banged his fist on the door and the moment Dr Morris opened the door, Jack grabbed him and shoved him up against the wall. Then he told him that the Russian mob or KGB were now giving him hassle because of what Dr Morris had told them and if the Professor had to suffer another visit like that again, he would not kill him, but he would make sure that Dr Morris would spend the rest of his days in a wheelchair, eating and shitting through a tube, and so, he should think twice about what he had gotten himself involved in.

Dr Morris started crying and said that he just wanted his wife back. Jack told him that it was impossible, because they no longer had a time machine and therefore he would simply have to accept that she was gone. Then Jack drove back to the Professor's and told him what he had done. And that he hoped they would never hear from him again, for Dr Morris own sake.

Jack spent the rest of the evening comforting Reynora, who was still in shock. He promised her that no harm would come to her as long as he was alive. Jack stayed at the Professor's to make sure that they were all safe.

The following day, Jack still wanted to stay with them, in case anybody turned up, but the Professor said that it would be better if he stayed at home, because it would harder for the university to sack him than Jack. The Professor told Jack not to worry because Reynora and her father would be safe as long as they stayed with him.

Jack cycled to work that morning, in case his new car was ready. He did not want to get stuck with two cars. After work, Jack went back to the Professor's house, but before entering, he noticed a mysterious car which he had not seen parked there before. He went inside and told the Professor about his observation. The Professor told Jack that he was aware of the car, but he did not want to make a fuss. Reynora was still in shock.

Jack suggested that they call the police, but the Professor was not keen on that idea, because the last time they called them, it had only made matters worse. Jack hoped that he and Reynora would have some time alone, but it would have to wait, because they spent the rest of the day and evening inside. Jack tried to teach her some of his language and to play games in order to make her feel more secure.

The following day, Jack cycled to work, and again, the Professor stayed at home with Reynora and her father. It was a quiet day at work as Jack continued his efforts to keep the students interested. He had received a call from the car dealer who let him know that his car was ready to be picked up. So, once he finished teaching, he went to get his new car. He was very excited about taking Reynora out for a spin.

When he arrived back at the Professor's, he drove past the house to check if the car from yesterday was still there. After a couple of trips up and down the road, he still had not noticed any mysterious cars parked where they shouldn't be, but as he entered the drive, both Reynora and her father were frightened that it may be some nasty people coming to hurt them.

The Professor laughed and told them that it was only Jack. And then they all went to look at his new car. Reynora walked over to Jack and slapped him, but she was also smiling. The Professor laughed and said, "You frightened them because you drove up in your new car and you hadn't told them about it."

Jack held Reynora close and explained that he had already promised her that nobody would harm her as long as he was alive. Then everybody got in the car and they went for a drive and when they returned, Jack noticed the mysterious car again. Without making a fuss, he told the Professor, who did not make a fuss either. Instead he brought Reynora and her father back inside the house, while Jack stayed outside. He told the Professor that he would investigate further. He pulled out of the driveway, drove around the corner and parked the car. He pulled the gun out from under the passenger seat and then walked back.

He sneaked up from behind, his hand on the gun. When he knocked on the car window, he could see that the people inside were not locals. They looked Russian. The men in the car quickly drove off. Jack ran after them but couldn't catch up. He wrote the license plate number down while he still remembered it. Then he walked back to his own car, but did not drive back until he got his breath back.

As he entered the house, they were busy cooking dinner, and Jack just said that he had taken care of business. And that was when the Professor started worrying, saying that they would have to come up with some sort of solution to their problem. Reynora came in from the kitchen and hugged Jack. Jack did everything he could to appear happy and make everything appear to be normal, because he did not want to upset her.

They all sat down to dinner, but it was a rather tense evening. Jack and the Professor tried not to show how worried they were, because they did not want Reynora and her father to know. Fortunately, the weekend was coming up and then Jack could spend all his time with Reynora and protect her if anybody tried any funny business.

On Thursday, Jack and the Professor tried to come up with a solution to all their problems. The Professor suggested that Reynora and her father should stay in his summerhouse, until things had settled down. But Jack opposed that idea, because if anything happened, they would be too far away.

The Professor said that he was able to take some days off work and he could go with them. Jack agreed that they would probably be safer there than here, he just wanted to make sure that nobody would follow them.

And so, he wanted the Professor to go by a different route, giving Jack the opportunity to check if anybody was following them. Then they would meet up at the road to the summerhouse, and Jack would continue to leave a few cars in between them, to make sure they were not being followed.

If, however, someone had placed a tracking device on either of their cars, they would have to get different cars. The criminals would still be able to find them in rental cars, so Jack suggested that they crash their cars and then they the garage would provide them with a car from while their cars were being repaired. Then they could use those cars to pick up Reynora and her father somewhere where there would be lots of people and they would blend in.

Jack and the Professor got in their cars, and while Jack was not happy about crashing his brand-new car, he believed that it would be worth it, to bring Reynora and her father to safety. Jack drove his car slowly into the Professor's and made a small dent in it. Then they drove to the garage to make sure they had other cars they could borrow.

The following day, Jack and the Professor left their own cars at the garage and drove off in two borrowed cars instead. They carried out their plan and fortunately, it would appear that they were not followed.

When they arrived at the Professor's summerhouse, Jack was pleased to see that it was surrounded by beautiful nature and a lush forest. It was a place just like this, he had hoped he would be able to take Reynora.

They spent the weekend relaxing and enjoying the wonderful surroundings. Jack had to call his parents and let them know that he would not come to see them on Sunday. They had such a good time that the weekend simply flew by and before they knew it, it was Monday, and Jack had to go to work.

It would be quite a while before Jack would see them again, but at least he knew that they were safe. Jack left the summerhouse and drove straight to work. He simply had to make the week pass as best he could, and then he would spend time with Reynora again.

Jack asked his brother James if he could borrow his car the coming Friday. But half way through the week, Jack was told by the garage that his and the Professor's cars were ready. The Professor drove down from the summerhouse and decided to check up on his house seeing as he was in town.

However, in order to make sure he was not followed, he decided to take the train back to the summerhouse. And on the Friday, Jack also had to use public transport to go to his brother's where he picked up another car. Then he drove to the summerhouse, constantly keeping an eye out in case some mysterious car was following him.

Reynora and Jack were so happy to be together again, and they spent every minute together. Saturday morning, as Jack and Reynora went shopping, Jack noticed a suspicious looking car. When they got back to the summerhouse, the car was still following them.

Jack ran to the Professor and told him what had happened. He took out his gun and went to investigate, but as he reached the car, he could tell that there were two people now, and so he hurried back and told the Professor that they had to get out of there and fast.

They all started packing their things, but it was too late. There were already two cars outside. They still managed to get into their own car and speed past the two strange cars, who turned around and started chasing them. Jack did everything he could to lose the cars in pursuit, but when he saw how frightened Reynora was, it was more than he could take. Nobody would ever be allowed to harm them. He managed to make a little headway with enough of a gap to drop off his passengers.

And then he turned around and drove towards the two cars. As the first car approached, he rolled down his window and pulled out his gun and shot at it. The first car was unprepared and could do nothing, but the other car could very well start shooting back at him. Jack had to try and hit the tires of the second car. But once the first car did a handbrake turn, the second followed suit. Jack wanted to aim at the tires and he hoped that if he hit them, the car would crash, and so he also made a handbrake turn, which meant he kept the other cars on the right side, and he was able to aim his gun at the tires.

Finally, he managed to hit the first car's tires, and the driver lost control as it flipped over and smashed into the second car. Jack stopped and walked over to the cars to check that the criminals were dead. Only, there was no need because within seconds both cars blew up. The petrol tanks had been leaking and a spark did the rest. The Police and Fire Department arrived and asked Jack what had happened, but he just told them that he didn't know.

Then he drove back to the others and they all drove back to the summerhouse to enjoy the rest of the weekend. That day, two CIA agents paid them a visit at the summerhouse. They said that they could not quite figure out how it all added up, but they were genuinely pleased that the KGB agents whom they had been after for years, were now dead and gone.

On the Sunday, the Professor and Reynora's father drove back into town, while Jack and Reynora went to see his family. Jack introduced them all to Reynora. And everybody was very pleased for him, because finally, he had found his dream-girl, and like he had once told his brother, she was out of this world, literally.

Jack managed to get a great career and a wonderful wife who made him happy and whom he would spend the rest of his life with. He saw the universe in a completely different way and he wondered what else was out there that nobody could possibly imagine.